"You're looking for a housemate?"

Elizabeth stared at Sam, still unable to believe he was actually standing in front of her. "Well, uh, yeah," she responded. "Jessica, Neil, and I."

What did Sam want from her? she wondered. If he was so interested in her life, why hadn't he gotten in touch with her?

"That's funny," Sam said, meeting her eyes, "because I'm looking for a place. I got wait listed for housing at my school. That's why I stopped by SVU—to see if anyone was looking to share an apartment."

"Oh, I don't—you mean—" Elizabeth stammered, racking her brain for a way to tell Sam that pigs would fly before she would live under the same roof with him.

Bantam Books in the Sweet Valley University series.
Ask your bookseller for the books you have missed.

And don't miss these Sweet Valley
University Thriller Editions:

Visit the Official Sweet Valley Web Site on the Internet at:

http://www.sweetvalley.com

SWEET VALLEY UNIVERSITY®

Living Together

Written by
Laurie John

Created by
FRANCINE PASCAL

BANTAM BOOKS
NEW YORK · TORONTO · LONDON · SYDNEY · AUCKLAND

RL 8, age 14 and up

LIVING TOGETHER
A Bantam Book / October 1999

Sweet Valley High® and Sweet Valley University®
are registered trademarks of Francine Pascal.
Conceived by Francine Pascal.

Produced by 17th Street Productions,
a division of Daniel Weiss Associates, Inc.
33 West 17th Street
New York, NY 10011.

ISBN: 0-553-49271-3

Published simultaneously in the United States and Canada

Bantam Books are published by Bantam Books, a division of Random
House, Inc. Its trademark, consisting of the words "Bantam Books" and
the portrayal of a rooster, is Registered in U.S. Patent and Trademark
Office and in other countries. Marca Registrada. Bantam Books, 1540
Broadway, New York, New York 10036.

PRINTED IN THE UNITED STATES OF AMERICA

OPM   0 9 8 7 6 5 4 3 2 1

To Anders Johansson

Chapter One

No parents.

No dorms.

No *room*mates.

No eagle-eyed RA.

No totally disgusting, mass-produced cafeteria food.

And no more being a lowly freshman!

Jessica Wakefield stood in front of 15 Crescent Road, giant suitcase in one hand, key in the other, staring at the incredibly cool duplex that was now her home.

I'm a sophomore and I have my own house! she wanted to scream at the top of her lungs. *My own house!*

Well, not her *own* house. She was sharing it with her two best friends: her twin sister, Elizabeth (who she didn't always get along with), and Neil Martin (the greatest guy in the world).

How cool was that!

And how cool was seeing their names on the black mailbox next to the front door?

E. Wakefield

J. Wakefield

N. Martin

That made it official. *Real*.

Dropping the heavy suitcase on the doorstep, Jessica unlocked the door and pushed it wide open.

Early afternoon sunlight streamed through the narrow windows on either side of the door and from a wide bay window that faced into the living room. Jessica walked inside and spun slowly around.

The duplex was totally empty, totally run-down . . . and totally great!

"I can't believe the slumlord didn't paint the place!" a male voice complained from behind her.

Jessica turned around to see Neil Martin putting down a huge cardboard box marked Kitchen Stuff and grimacing as he picked a chip of white paint off the peeling, scuffed wall. "If we get stuck painting ourselves, he'd better knock some money off next month's rent."

"I can totally picture it!" Jessica exclaimed. "A buttery yellow, or maybe a really cool lavender, and we can stencil—"

"*Jess*—" Elizabeth Wakefield groaned as she staggered through the doorway, her arms anchored by two bulging suitcases. "Forget the color scheme and help unload the U-Haul. We have about a million boxes left to unpack. And get your suitcase out of the doorway—I almost tripped over it."

Jessica rolled her eyes at her identical twin. Although they were only four minutes apart in age, Elizabeth had an annoying tendency to act like she was thirty instead of nineteen.

"The U-Haul can wait for five minutes, Liz," Jessica said, surveying the living room. "Let's explore a little. We barely got to check the place out with that realtor breathing down our necks."

Without bothering to wait for Elizabeth's expected "no, Jess, *now*," Jessica headed through a swinging door and found herself in the kitchen. The small, sunny room had sliding glass doors that opened onto a tiny, scraggly backyard enclosed by a fence. Maybe Elizabeth could take up gardening.

A slab of counter jutted out into the center of the room, lined by round metal stools that were set into the floor. Jessica sat down on one of the stools and tried to push off, but the stool didn't swivel.

Neil came through the swinging door, took one look at her pout, and said, "Doesn't spin, huh? That blows."

Jessica grinned. Neil always could read her mind. If she didn't already have a twin, she'd think she and Neil had been separated at birth. It figured that the one guy she was completely comfortable with and found incredibly cute was . . . gay!

She shot off the stool and started opening cupboards. All of them were bare and a little dusty. There was something invigorating about all that empty space. *Clean slate. Chance to start fresh.* She, Elizabeth, and Neil were really starting from scratch. And that was exactly what Jessica wanted to do this year.

"So you really like this place that much, huh?" Neil asked.

"Like it? I *love* it!" Jessica gave Neil a hug. "And you know what? This is going to be a *great* party house."

Neil laughed. "Yeah, like a *year* from now, Jess. This place is really run-down."

"It's not run-down—it's *charming*. As soon as we finish moving our stuff in and get some living-room furniture from a thrift store, this place will look amazing." Jessica flitted around the kitchen, twisting faucets on and off, opening and shutting drawers. She peered into the refrigerator. "Hey, the light's broken."

"More like the *electricity's* broken," Neil said. "We have to get the utilities turned on."

"Oh, yeah. I knew that." Jessica shut the refrigerator door. Okay, so in addition to no parents, no dorm rules, and no bad cafeteria food, there would be no blow drying, at least until tomorrow.

"But wait, there's more," Neil went on.

"Other than the electricity—which we can't do anything about today because it's Sunday—there's painting, and cleaning, and oh, yeah—finding a fourth housemate. And we have to do all that stuff right away."

"Okay, okay—so we have a lot to do," Jessica said. "So we'll do it."

Neil raised an eyebrow and smiled. "That's right, Jess. *We'll* do it."

A year ago she would have tuned Neil out, the way she tuned out Elizabeth or her parents or anyone else who tried to give her a reality check. But Jessica couldn't pretend anymore that if she ignored unpleasant stuff, it would just go away (or that Elizabeth would deal with it).

Of course she knew the apartment was more than just a place to party. It meant being independent. Taking care of her own life instead of leaving it to other people.

That was a little scary. But it was exactly what she wanted. For her sophomore year at Sweet Valley University, she was determined to act more like an adult, to take life more seriously. To be a little bit more like Elizabeth.

Now *that* was really scary!

"It won't be that much work split three ways," Neil said, clearly noticing that Jessica's smile had gone down a few watts.

"Four ways," Jessica corrected.

"That's right," Neil agreed, his gorgeous gray

5

eyes twinkling. "And we'll make whoever moves in deal with everything."

Jessica laughed and felt herself getting psyched again.

"Liz!" Jessica's voice floated through the duplex as Elizabeth lugged a stereo speaker into the living room. "We need you to settle something. I say this is a closet, and Neil says it's a bedroom!"

"Just give me a minute." Elizabeth set down the speaker and wiped the sweat from her forehead. That third trip out to the U-Haul had left her winded. She caught her breath, finally taking a minute to look around.

Okay, so the duplex was a little run-down. And it seemed a little smaller than she remembered. But there was something charming about all the quaint details, like the bay window with its hardwood seat and the stairs' carved hardwood banister. Elizabeth tried to picture herself curled up in the window seat, reading, or coming down those stairs in the morning.

It was a little strange to think of herself living in this space, of her life unfolding within these walls.

She got up and walked around the room, gazing up at the ceiling and out the windows. Her mind drifted back to her first day at Sweet Valley U, how she'd wandered around like this in an empty dorm room in Dickenson Hall, full of excitement, hope, and the jitters.

"Isn't it wild?" Jessica's face emerged from the doorway she had disappeared through ten minutes ago. "All this space is *ours!*"

Elizabeth smiled as she shut the door of the closet she'd been peering into. "I know. I can't quite believe that I'm standing in *my* living room in *my* house. I still haven't gotten used to the fact that we're starting a new school year."

And stranger yet, Elizabeth realized, she was starting it alone. Meaning, no boyfriend.

"No kidding," Jessica agreed. "I feel like we just finished with finals two weeks ago. There's no way we're sophomores already."

"Yeah, no way," Elizabeth agreed, realizing that she'd zeroed in on what had been bothering her all day. It wasn't that she was in a strange place, or was anxious about starting sophomore year, or even that everything she owned was buried in boxes.

It was knowing that she was on her own. Last year she and Tom Watts had been an inseparable couple. And now she was . . .

On her own. How long had it been since she was truly independent . . . without a boyfriend to fall back on? Even this past summer, when she was grappling with the realization that it was really over with Tom, she'd been distracted by . . . Sam.

A distraction was *all* he'd been, Elizabeth

reminded herself. Obviously their time together had meant nothing to him, or he would have bothered to return her calls and her letter. But she should have known all his talk of staying friends was just lip service. Sam wasn't exactly the most dependable guy. At this point she never expected to hear from him again.

"Earth to Liz." Jessica waved both hands in front of Elizabeth's face. "You zoned for a minute."

Elizabeth shrugged, any explanation seeming inadequate. "I'm just . . . still getting my bearings."

"Oh." Jessica looked at her. "Well . . . I'll leave you alone for a little while, then. I'm going to scope out the second floor." Like a shot, Jessica hurtled up the stairs.

Elizabeth dropped onto the window seat with a sigh, crossing her arms over her body. Sometimes she envied Jessica. Her sister was so dynamic, so adaptable, whereas Elizabeth was thrown by transitions. While Jessica was in heaven over their new house, Elizabeth was obsessing about everything they still had to do to get settled in.

What if they couldn't find a fourth roommate right away? What if they'd been stupid to take a place the three of them couldn't afford? What if they were short on rent and actually had to ask Mr. and Mrs. Wakefield for more money? Elizabeth had already lost a few nights of sleep worrying about possibilities that probably hadn't even occurred to her twin.

Granted, Jessica got herself into a lot more trouble than Elizabeth, with her tendency to leap before she looked. But Jessica always seemed to land on her feet.

"Liz, come quick!" Jessica screamed from upstairs, a bloodcurdling scream that had Elizabeth sprinting up the stairs in a second.

Todd Wilkins dropped his gym bag, tiptoed down the hall, and sneaked up behind Dana Upshaw. He pressed his chest against her back and covered her eyes with his palms. "Guess who?" he whispered in her ear.

His breath was still coming in shallow gasps from his trip to the gym, but he couldn't resist the chance to surprise his girlfriend.

Dana leaned back against Todd. He could feel the fringe of her eyelashes fluttering against his palms. "Mmmm . . . let me guess. Is it someone really sweaty?"

"What gave me away?" Todd let his hands slide to Dana's shoulders, then he spun her gently around.

As he grinned into Dana's gorgeous hazel eyes, everything but the two of them receded far away. The stereo blasting through Dana's off-campus apartment, the clatter of her housemates making brunch in the kitchen . . . it all belonged to some distant background. Nothing existed for Todd but Dana's smile, her perfect skin, the perfume he'd bought her last week just because it was Wednesday. . . .

She looked totally hot in her cutoff jean shorts and pale pink tank top, her thick, long, curly mahogany hair tumbling down her back. Todd was convinced she got more gorgeous every day. He'd been crashing at her place for two weeks now, and every day he still rushed straight home (from the gym) just to see her face.

Although it was a hassle to live out of a duffel bag, Todd was actually a little glad he'd missed the deadline for the housing lottery. There was nowhere he'd rather be living than right here with Dana.

"You know," Todd said in a low voice, wrapping his arms around Dana's waist, "I've been at the gym pumping iron so you won't dump me for some guy who could kick my butt. You don't mind a little sweat, do you?"

Dana squeezed Todd's bicep and pressed her lips together. "Hmmm . . . Okay, I guess I can forgive you."

Todd unzipped his sweatshirt and tossed it aside, then peeled off his T-shirt. He twirled the shirt on his fingertip in a mock striptease before flinging it on the floor. "But first, behold my studliness!" He puffed up his chest and made ridiculous muscle-man poses. "And now you will be mine!"

Dana cracked up as Todd chased her down the hall toward her bedroom. She raced into the room and bounced onto the bed. Todd paused in the doorway to kick off his sneakers and socks. "I've got you now!" He shut the door behind them, then lunged at the bed and pounced on top of her.

After a moment Dana stopped giggling, and the look in her eyes turned smoldering. Todd gazed down at her flushed face for a moment, then lowered his lips to hers for a soft, lingering kiss.

The door to Dana's room banged open. Todd rolled away from Dana to see Molly, one of Dana's housemates, standing in the doorway. Molly's eyes were blazing, and her hands were planted on her hips.

"First of all," Molly snapped, "could you two keep the noise down? It's really nauseating to listen to the two of you act out scenes from some romance novel at top volume."

Todd and Dana exchanged sheepish looks. "But Dana's just so cute that I can't help saying adorable things to her," Todd said, putting his arm around Dana's neck. He flashed Molly his most endearing aren't-I-the-perfect-boyfriend smile, the one that always made Dana's housemates start *awwwing*.

But Molly's jaw was set in an irate line. "*Second* of all, *Todd*," she continued, "could you please *stop* throwing your sweaty, disgusting gym stuff all over our floor? There are three people who live here who *don't* like sharing your germs."

Todd's jaw dropped. Where did she get off, talking to him that way? He glared at Molly. "For your informa—"

"Sorry, Molly," Dana interrupted. "You're absolutely right—we'll try to keep Todd's stuff in my room."

"Thank you," Molly said. "But do better than *try*," she added before slamming the door on her way out. Todd rolled his eyes at Dana.

"That girl's got a serious attitude problem," Todd said. "Now, where were we?" He propped himself up on his elbow and gazed at Dana. "Just wait till I'm a star point guard for the Lakers," he murmured, tracing the line of her jaw with his fingertip. "I'll buy us our own mansion—a hundred rooms that nobody will be allowed to barge into. What would you say to being a kept woman?" He grinned.

But Dana didn't smile back. "Todd, it *is* asking kind of a lot of my roommates to have a fifth person staying here. They're used to it since we had another housemate last year, but I'm sure they'd feel better if they knew you're really trying to find a place. How's the search coming—any leads?"

Todd swallowed hard. The truth was, he'd been so content staying here with Dana that he'd barely bothered to scan the classifieds. "I have a few calls to make," he said. That was *sort of* true— since he hadn't made a single call, he was certainly long overdue to make a few.

"Well, let me know if there's anything I can do to help," Dana said, looking a little worried. "But you'd better get moving—everyone's starting to come back for the fall semester. Pretty soon everything decent will be taken."

"I'll find something. Don't worry," Todd assured her.

But a nagging doubt tugged at him as he planted a kiss in her hair. Dana was right—he was probably too late to find a decent apartment, just like he'd been too late for the housing lottery. Todd just couldn't psych himself up to look for a place. In fact, he wasn't really looking forward to any aspect of the new school year. All he really cared about was spending every spare minute with Dana.

"Tina? Tina, right?"

Nina Harper looked up to see a vaguely familiar blond girl in a pink Kappa Delta Gamma sweatshirt blocking her way in the lobby of Dickenson Hall. Nina lifted her knee to hoist the minifridge she was carrying and repositioned her hands to get a better grip on it. "It's *Nina*," she grunted. *Can't you see I'm in the middle of heavy lifting?* she added mentally.

"Oh, right, *Nina!*" The girl sounded

unnaturally excited to see someone whose name she couldn't remember. "Remember me? Carrie Cranshaw—I lived on your floor last year?"

"Um, yeah," Nina said. Carrie was still blocking her path, and Nina's fingers felt like they were about to break under the minifridge. She leaned the appliance against the corridor wall to relieve herself of some weight.

"Can you believe we're actually sophomores?" Carrie went on obliviously. Nina noticed that Carrie's ponytail bounced up and down when she talked. "We're going to have sooo much more fun this year now that we're not freshmen!"

Why was this girl blabbing on and on to her? Nina wondered. It wasn't like they'd ever exchanged more than polite hellos. Carrie existed in a completely different circle. Nina wasn't the type who came to college to party—she'd never even understood how those people managed to function.

Granted, most of them probably weren't physics majors, like Nina. She barely had time to get her work done and sleep—partying with the Greek Row crowd wasn't even a possibility. Not that she'd fit in with them anyway. Nina never hung out with anyone from the dorms—except Elizabeth. But they hadn't kept in touch over the summer, and now Elizabeth was living in her own house off campus.

"This is going to be so great—just like old

times!" Carrie went on. "*Everybody* from last year is here. I've seen Donna and Kim and Steph and—and you, Tina! Oh, and did I mention I was running for dorm president? I have really great ideas for Dickenson. . . ."

Nina, Nina corrected mentally, tuning out Carrie and easing the fridge back into her arms. Now she understood why Carrie was being Ms. Friendly. Nina huffed air upward to blow a stray lock of her bangs out of her eyes.

"You know, we should totally hang out more—get to know each other better," Carrie said as Nina started to move past her.

Yeah, right, Nina thought. *Until voting day for dorm president. After that, you won't even remember what my name* rhymes *with.*

It *would* be nice to make a few real friends, though, she thought. She was usually too busy studying to hang out with anyone. Maybe she should try not to be so obsessed with work this year. Maybe getting to know her floor mates would take her mind off . . . stuff.

"Hey, how come that cutie I always saw you with last year isn't carrying that heavy fridge for you? What was his name—Ryan, right?" Carrie flashed a very bright, fake smile.

Bryan, Nina corrected silently, unable to keep her own fake smile plastered on her face for another second. *And thanks for reminding me, Barrie. Oops, I mean,* Carrie. "You're right—this

15

fridge *is* really heavy," Nina said. "I'd better get moving, or my arms will break. Talk to you some other time."

Like never, Nina added to herself as she pushed past Carrie. Nina had been right in the first place—she was here to work. And socializing was definitely *not* going to make her life easier.

Chloe Murphy caught a last anxious glimpse of herself in the rearview mirror as her taxi pulled up in front of Oakley Hall. Her brownish matte lipstick (no other makeup, of course) looked perfectly retro cool. Her faded black armylike tank top and worn, baggy gray cords (no belt) looked perfectly minimal cool. As did her I-spent-an-hour-to-get-it-to-look-this-way flat, seemingly unwashed auburn hair. And last year's black leather slides, just beat up enough, looked perfectly trendy cool.

She looked perfectly imperfect. Okay, she was ready. The moment of truth.

Chloe was going to be who *she* wanted to be. Self-sufficient. Her own person. Judged by who she was—not by how much money her family had. Her family's money had dictated who she was for too long. Chloe figured that if no one at SVU knew she came from a very wealthy family, then no one could peg her as this or that; she could forge her own identity. The way she was dressed today was exactly how she felt inside and the way she wanted to be perceived: down-to-earth.

She handed the driver the fare, then slung her duffel bag and backpack over her shoulder and slid out of the cab.

At the top of the Oakley Hall steps Chloe took a deep breath before pushing through the heavy double doors. Inside, clusters of girls swarmed around the lobby, their excited voices echoing across the glass-paneled walls.

Chloe's stomach fluttered with the sudden flash that these were the people she would be *living* with—maybe for the next few years. What if they didn't like her? What if they thought she was about as cool as pajamas with feet?

A tall girl lugging a cardboard box pushed past Chloe, almost knocking her over. Reunions were taking place over piles of luggage; the lobby was like an obstacle course. Chloe flattened herself against the wall to sidle past a sprawling group of sorority types hugging one another and jumping up and down. "I missed you too!" they were all chirping.

Everybody seemed to know one another already, Chloe noted. *And where is the B wing anyway?* she wondered. The letter she'd received from the housing office had said to report to the third-floor lounge in wing B for her room assignment and key. But no one was even acknowledging her existence, and since everyone was moving around so fast or talking to someone,

Chloe didn't feel comfortable asking anyone for directions.

She finally saw the small sign for the B wing just as she was about to work up the guts to actually speak to someone. Chloe followed the arrows, wondering why no one else looked as lost and alone as Chloe felt. *This is your first day at college. Cut yourself a break,* she told herself. She had to give herself time. All these girls had been freshmen once. Pretty soon Chloe would fit right in with everybody.

I sound like a Seventeen *article on surviving being a freshman,* Chloe realized. *But please let it be true.*

Chloe stopped in front of the elevator and pushed the up button. When the doors opened, a curly-haired girl got in after Chloe and smiled. "You look familiar. Did you live on the third floor last year?"

Chloe beamed her friendliest smile. "No, actually . . . I wasn't here last year. I'm a freshman."

"Oh." The flicker of interest went out of the girl's eyes at the word *freshman*. The doors opened for the third floor, and the girl pushed her way out without another word.

Chloe followed, staring at the ground, feeling stupid. It wasn't about her, she told herself. As soon as she found a bunch of freshmen girls, they'd be insta-bonding over how left out the upperclassmen made them feel.

Please let that be true too.

Luckily the lounge was directly across from the elevator bank. A bunch of girls stood around, wearing Oakley baseball caps and carrying clipboards. Chloe went up to the girl wearing the baseball cap with *M–P* pasted across it.

She waited her turn, then told the girl her name.

"Murphy, Chloe," the girl said, trailing down the list of names on her clipboard. "There you are—Chloe Murphy, room 30. That's down the hall, to the left. Here's your key. Welcome to Oakley," the girl added, looking behind Chloe to help the next girl.

Friendly, Chloe thought, fingering the key as she walked down the hall. In front of the closed door marked room 30, Chloe took a deep breath. She pulled at her tank top until it was a little more slouchy. If her mother could see what she was wearing right now, she'd probably faint from the shock. But Chloe wasn't living by her mother's rules anymore. *Thank God.*

As she gripped the doorknob to insert her key, she realized too late that the door was already unlocked. She practically fell into her dorm room, staggering several steps to avoid collapsing under the weight of her duffel bag.

And she found herself staring into a pair of cold green eyes. A girl lay sprawled across a satin-quilted bed by the window, looking completely relaxed and at home.

"Nice entrance," the girl said, every syllable full of biting sarcasm. "I'm Moira Pierce. You must be my rooomie."

"Chloe Murphy." Chloe took a step forward and tentatively outstretched her hand toward Moira, then tried to busy herself with her duffel bag when it became obvious that Moira wasn't the hand-shaking type. "I, uh . . . hi." She could feel her face flushing.

"I hope you don't mind me taking the window side," Moira continued in a flat tone. "We New Yorkers are really sensitive to light. Your bed's behind the door."

Chloe closed the door and looked at the bare cot that was awkwardly positioned in the corner of the room. "That's okay," she said brightly. "You were here first. The early bird catches the worm, right?"

Chloe winced the second the words were out of her mouth. *The early bird?* What had possessed her to say that? *Moira must think I'm an idiot already,* Chloe decided.

Moira just nodded slowly, her green eyes narrowed. Chloe held her breath as her room-mate's even gaze raked up and down her carefully chosen outfit. Moira had the air of someone who'd seen it all, been everywhere, done everything. She probably thought Chloe was totally unsophisti-cated and uncool—and at the moment Chloe couldn't blame her.

Finally Moira's lips curled into something like a sneer. "Those shoes are Prada, right?" she asked.

"Uh . . . no, of course not. They're just rip-offs." Chloe felt her face flame bright red to the tips of her ears. She'd decided to keep the shoes because she didn't think anyone would expect a freshman to have real designer shoes.

"I know Prada when I see it," Moira said.

Just my luck, Chloe thought.

Chapter Two

"What are you two fighting about?" Neil poked his head into the doorway of a huge second-floor room, where the twins stood glaring at each other.

"Jess screamed bloody murder and scared me half to death," Elizabeth panted. "I ran all the way upstairs only to find that the emergency was Jessica deciding this was *her* room."

Jessica stretched out her arms, tilted back her chin, and twirled around the bedroom. "Well, look at it! How gorgeous is this?" She gestured out the large bay window identical to the one downstairs, where the afternoon sun hung low in the sky.

"Yeah, it's gorgeous, but that doesn't make it yours!" Elizabeth exclaimed. "I'm paying just as much rent as you, so why shouldn't *I* get this room?"

"And check *this* out!" Ignoring her sister, Jessica ran across the hardwood floor and slid open a shuttered door, revealing a walk-in closet. "I'll be able to fit all my stuff in here!"

"I'll be able to fit all *my* stuff in there," Elizabeth said.

"Did it occur to either of you that *I* might want this room too?" Neil asked.

"Like either of you has as many clothes, shoes, and bags as I do," Jessica said with a dismissive wave of her hand. "So I should get it. Plus I saw it first. I already feel like it's mine."

"You saw it first?" Elizabeth mimicked. "Jess, we're not six years old. Having our own place is a huge responsibility—you have to start acting like a grown-up!"

Neil covered his face with his hand. He loved the Wakefield twins—Jessica was like a sister to him—but they could drive him totally crazy. They had such opposite personalities and such strong wills. Neil felt like he had to shout to be heard—or give up altogether.

Shout it was. "Listen!" Neil yelled, momentarily silencing the bickering twins. "Neither one of you is getting the room without a fight. I've checked out the other rooms, and this one is definitely the primo real estate. The one down the hall is a decent size, but then there's just that shoe box by the kitchen and a musty, dusty old attic room."

"I'm not living in an attic," Jessica declared.

24

"Well, *I'm* not living by the kitchen," Elizabeth put in. "I can't be in a high-traffic area. I'd never get any work done."

Neil groaned. "We can each pick a room and then give whichever one's left over to the fourth person."

"You've got that right," Jessica agreed. "But that still doesn't leave enough *good* rooms to go around. And I'm not giving up this one."

"Well, neither am I!" Elizabeth was talking louder and louder. "You can't honestly believe you deserve this room because you have more shoes than I do!"

Neil slumped against the door frame and silently counted to ten. Sometimes it boggled his mind just how naive Jessica and Elizabeth could be. He'd only known them since the summer, when they'd all participated in the Intense Cable Sports Network's big summer Coast-to-Coast Road Trip competition. None of them had won the scholarship prize, but Neil had gotten very close to the Wakefields. All summer he'd been impressed by the strength Jessica hid under her borderline flighty exterior and by the reason and compassion Elizabeth always exhibited in a crisis.

But ever since they'd started talking about getting a place together, Neil had worried that the twins weren't taking it seriously enough—like this was all a fun extension of their summer adventure together. He didn't know how to get it through to them that having their own place wasn't about a big bedroom or storing shoes.

"All right, break it up, you two!" Neil made a T shape with his hands. "I want this room as much as you guys do. But we still have about a million boxes to unload. So we'd better get moving if we're going to squeeze in a trip to get furniture before we have to bring the U-Haul back." He backed through the doorway, gesturing at them to follow.

"Neil's right, Jess." Elizabeth lifted her chin and gave her sister a cool stare. "We can discuss this like *adults* later." She headed after Neil.

Neil glanced over his shoulder at Elizabeth, stifling the unkind urge to ask what she knew about being an adult when Mr. and Mrs. Wakefield were paying her and Jessica's rent. Neil was the only member of this household who was really on his own. Not that he took any particular pride in that fact—it was just that since he came out to his parents, he really didn't have any other options.

His parents weren't into financially supporting his *lifestyle*. But it didn't take money to be gay. It took money to pay for tuition, textbooks, rent, food. . . .

He couldn't really hold it against the twins that they were in a better financial situation than he was. He was grateful that they'd agreed to go in on the apartment with him—he could never afford a place of his own.

But the fact remained that he had a lot more at stake than they did. They'd managed to float the first month's rent and security three ways, assuming that they could quickly find a fourth roommate who'd reimburse them for his or her share. And while Jessica and Elizabeth could always call Mommy and Daddy in a pinch, Neil had nobody to turn to. If he ended up having to eat that first month's third of the rent, well . . . he wouldn't be eating anything else for weeks.

Some senior year this is going to be, Tom Watts thought, setting down a plastic milk crate full of CDs on the floor of his dorm room at Reid Hall. He and Elizabeth were history; his best friend, Danny, wasn't coming back to SVU this year, and Tom wasn't really into devoting every waking moment of his senior year to being a journalist for the campus TV station.

What had happened to him? he wondered. Journalism had been his whole life, his great passion. But now things were different. He was different.

What am I going to do with this year, supposedly the best year of college?

He grabbed a Coke out of the minifridge and sat down on the twin-sized bed, which was a foot too short for him. At least he had a single—his own room—a major upperclassman perk.

"Wildman Watts!" a huge voice boomed. "I thought that was you!"

Lance Travis, one of Tom's old buddies from his football days, stood in the doorway. *Wildman*—it had been a long time since he'd heard that nickname.

"Hey, man, good to see you." Tom obligingly high-fived Lance's upturned palm. "I just finished moving in my stuff."

"No *way*, dude!" All six-foot-two, two-hundred-plus pounds of Lance's frame reeled. "I can't believe it—I live two doors down! Wildman Watts on my floor? That rocks!"

"Thanks, man." Tom felt an embarrassed smile spreading across his face. His quarterback days were long gone; he'd forgotten how it felt to be treated like a campus celebrity. Lance had been more of a drinking buddy than a close friend, and Tom hadn't even spoken to him in months—yet the guy was acting like he'd just run into Michael Jordan.

"You're a legend! The team hasn't been the same since you left. It's been, what, two seasons of sucking!" Lance clapped Tom on the back. "Listen, man, when we get done moving in, let me buy you a beer."

"Sounds good," Tom told him. "I'll knock on your door later." They exchanged high fives again, and Lance took off.

It wasn't like Tom was planning to get back in with the jock crowd—that scene wasn't really him anymore. He'd grown up a lot since his star-athlete days. Man, he had been full of himself then.

Still, maybe it would be cool to feel that way again. It was just one night, after all.

"Hello, I'm calling about the one bedroom?" Todd said, twirling the phone cord around his finger.

There was a sound like a snort on the other end of the line. "You gotta be kidding me," a gruff male voice said. "That ad was in *yesterday's* paper. At that price it got snapped up in ten minutes."

"Thanks anyway," Todd said. He hung up the phone and bent once more over the newspaper that was spread out on Dana's coffee table.

Somewhere down the hall a door creaked open. "*Todd,* are you *off* the phone yet?" The voice of Dana's housemate Kimiko echoed through the living room.

"*Yes!*" Todd shouted back. Kimiko's door slammed shut. "I was on for all of five seconds," Todd muttered to himself in irritation. It was no wonder he hadn't found a place yet, when he couldn't even get a minute of privacy to make a call.

Halfheartedly he scanned the tight columns of print he'd already pored over for hours. It was hopeless—there was nothing else in his price range. Todd had circled only three listings, and all of them were already rented.

"Todd, can I clue you in to something?" Molly strode into the living room, once again wearing her take-no-prisoners expression. "It might surprise you to learn that women do not swoon at the sexy sight of razor stubble in the sink."

"I didn't—," Todd protested.

"Nor do we consider it evidence of masculinity when you leave the toilet seat up," Molly went on. "In fact, we find it *rude* and *inconsiderate!*"

"Oh, come *on*." Todd groaned. "What is it with women and the seat? Just put it down—it's not that big a deal!"

He'd meant it as a joke, but the words came out sounding more snappish than Todd had intended. He knew instantly he'd crossed a line. Molly stood rigidly in the middle of the room, staring at Todd as if he were a cockroach crawling on her food.

"Let's get something straight, Todd," she said finally. "*I* pay rent in this apartment. So don't *you* tell me what is or isn't a big deal. Dana's my friend, but if you want to stay here, you'd better start being a little more respectful—and a little more hygienic."

Todd cringed as Molly turned and stalked out of the living room. He was totally busted. As long as he couldn't afford his own place, he had to bend over backward to stay on Dana's housemates' good side.

He skulked to the bathroom and ran water in

30

the sink, splashing water on the dark ring of razor stubble. Okay, so he could see how some of his habits were kind of gross by girl standards. He had to do something to make it up to them. Maybe he'd make everyone a big dinner—a gesture to show how much he appreciated their letting him stay here.

Feeling pleased with himself, Todd turned off the faucets and headed for the kitchen to make a shopping list. A nice meal and a little wine would smooth things over. When Dana's housemates saw he was making an effort, they'd chill out. Besides, he was bound to find an affordable apartment eventually. It wasn't like he would be imposing on them forever.

"One, two, three—*lift!*" Neil commanded. Elizabeth didn't think she had the energy to lift even her finger, but she, Jessica, their brother, Steven, and Neil hefted with all their might. The couch they'd just bought at the Salvation Army, a 1970s-style daisy-patterned monstrosity that Elizabeth had been outvoted on, lifted just enough to clear the threshold of the duplex. Together the four of them staggered forward a few paces into the living room.

"Which way?" Steven grunted.

Jessica vigorously inclined her head. "Middle of the room."

"No way!" Neil objected. "Over by the stairs."

31

"That makes no sense!" Jessica exclaimed. "Don't you know anything about *feng shui?*"

"*Feng* who?" Steven panted.

"Well, whoever he is, he's not the one who has to live here," Neil growled.

Straining under the weight of the couch, Elizabeth felt like her arms were about to be ripped from their sockets. "Will you guys just pick a spot?" she yelled in frustration. "We can always move it later."

"Okay, okay," Neil grumbled. "Let's just put it in the middle for now."

Painstakingly they inched the sofa forward and deposited it in the center of the room. Elizabeth eased her weary arms out from underneath the couch and gradually uncurled her stiff, swollen fingers.

Neil was frowning at the couch. "You know, it doesn't look half bad here," he admitted.

"It's perfect," Jessica declared. "Oooh, I have such a good idea. I'll be right back." She disappeared up the stairs.

Elizabeth plopped down onto the couch and eased off her tennis shoes. "Thanks for helping out, Steven."

"Yeah, we owe you one," Neil said.

"No sweat." Steven yanked playfully on Elizabeth's ponytail. "I'm going to get a drink from the kitchen. Anyone want anything?"

"All we have is tap water," Neil said.

"I think there's a box marked Glasses on the counter," Elizabeth called after her brother.

Jessica's clogs were clattering down the stairs. "Okay, it took me forever, but I found it!" She arrived in the living room holding up a long string of fairy lights with bulbs shaped like little daisies. "See, they match the couch! Neil, will you help me plug these in?"

"Uh, Jess, I think you're forgetting something," Neil said. "And besides, this is a living room, not a Christmas tree. Those lights are totally tacky."

"They're not tacky—they're *kitschy!*" Jessica said in a hurt voice. "Liz, don't you think the lights are cool?"

Elizabeth looked from her sister to Neil. She honestly didn't mind the lights, but she didn't want Neil to feel like the twins were ganging up on him. "We could see how they look and take them down if we don't like them," she suggested.

"What a shame that we *can't* see how they look because we don't have any *electricity* yet," Neil said. He folded his arms across his chest. "And they clash with my hula-girl lamp."

"Oh, my daisies are tacky, but your lamp isn't?" Jessica snorted. "*Hel*-lo."

"My lamp is campy," Neil said in a dignified voice. "Those lights don't quite cross the line between cheese and camp."

Elizabeth sighed in exasperation. "Look, you

33

guys, what difference does it make? It's not like we're having Martha Stewart over for dinner. As far as I'm concerned, we're all entitled to put whatever we want in the living room. We have more important stuff to worry about than interior decorating."

"Yeah, like finding a housemate," Neil pointed out. "I guess we'll just have to weed out anyone who gets seizures from staring at blinking daisy lights—if we even have electricity tomorrow."

Jessica looked like she was about to retort something vicious, but just then Steven reappeared in the living room, holding a mug. "Just so you guys know, there's no hot water," he reported. "And you may need to run the cold water for a few minutes until it turns from brown to clear."

Elizabeth groaned. "Great. One more thing to deal with. What did I do with my checklist?" She halfheartedly glanced around the living room for the notebook where she'd been jotting to-dos, but it was impossible to find anything in the sea of boxes that surrounded them.

"You and your checklist." Jessica rolled her eyes. "Our most basic need right now is food. I'm about to pass out from starvation. Who wants to split a pizza?"

"I'm starved too," Neil said.

Elizabeth nodded. "I'm in. Steven?"

"Thanks, but I'm meeting a couple of friends

for dinner," Steven said, heading for the door. "See you later, guys."

"Okay, pizza!" Jessica said. "Where's the phone?"

Elizabeth started to glance around, then cringed. No phone.

They all seemed to realize it at the same time. Steven laughed. "I can't believe you guys didn't call the phone company last week to get the line turned on."

"I'm glad you find that so funny," Jessica muttered.

One more thing to add to the to-do list, Elizabeth thought. If she could even *find* the list. Totally exhausted, Elizabeth realized all she wanted was to relax, not think another second about all the stuff they still had to do.

Elizabeth dragged herself to her feet. "You guys can go eat if you want," she said, plodding toward the staircase. "I'm going to take a shower and a quick nap."

"Oh, no, you don't," Jessica called after her. "Napping definitely constitutes marking territory. Nobody so much as shuts an eye until we decide on bedrooms."

"All *right*," Elizabeth snapped over her shoulder. "Do you mind if I take a shower, O Almighty One?"

"Of course not!" Jessica's voice was sugary sweet. "Go right ahead. Enjoy your cold, brown shower in the dark."

Elizabeth froze with her hand on the banister, cringing. She wanted to crumple to her feet and burst into tears then and there. This was really too much to bear. How could a simple thing like moving be so overwhelming?

"So, Chloe." Moira was perched on the edge of her bed, filing her nails. "Are you a freshman?"

Chloe froze in the middle of rifling through her duffel bag. Uh-oh. The *F* word. "Yeah," she admitted as casually as she could. "Aren't you?"

Forcing herself to keep breathing, Chloe fished a handful of black cotton underwear out of her duffel bag and dumped it into a dresser drawer. She was glad to be unpacking so she didn't have to meet Moira's intimidating gaze. Just looking into her roommate's eyes still made Chloe's heart hammer.

"Actually, I'm a sophomore." Moira blew on her nails, then stretched out her arm and studied her fanned fingertips. "I took a year off to do a fashion internship in New York, and when I came back, I got the dregs of the housing pool."

Chloe grimaced to herself as she transferred a ratty plaid flannel shirt to a drawer. Great. So there was an age difference between them. No wonder Chloe felt like such a dweeb around her roommate.

She stole a glance at Moira's superchic outfit. She should have guessed Moira studied fashion—she was so put together. Moira had the kind of style and sophistication money couldn't buy. Chloe wondered if she would ever possess that kind of poise. Even if Chloe did dress up in the kind of clothes her mother always bought for her, she'd still look *wrong*.

"Sooo, Chloe," Moira drawled again. "Are you a sunny California girl? Mommy and Daddy close enough to visit on weekends?"

Something about the tone of Moira's get-to-know-you banter reminded Chloe of a cat batting a fear-paralyzed mouse between its paws. "We . . . moved around a lot," Chloe said carefully. "Right now my parents live on the East Coast." That was about as detailed as she wanted to get. She didn't need to mention the Park Avenue apartment in New York City or the houses in Greenwich, Connecticut; Aspen; South Hampton; and South Beach, Florida.

Her hands encountered something soft and smooth in the duffel bag. Chloe glanced down and realized that the white silk blouse she'd worn at her high-school graduation was folded neatly between T-shirts. How had that gotten in there? She certainly didn't remember packing it.

Moira was asking her something. "Uh—sorry?" Chloe stammered, flustered. Beneath another T-shirt was a gray cashmere designer sweater. Her mother must have sneaked it all into her bag when she wasn't looking, Chloe realized. How *could* she? This was really going too far.

"I *asked* you where you went to high school," Moira repeated with pointed impatience.

"Uh, Winterbourne Academy," Chloe said, wadding the silk blouse into a ball. She turned to the dresser with her back to Moira and stuffed the blouse into the back of the drawer.

"Reeeally," Moira said in an ominous voice. "Impressive."

Chloe whirled and looked at Moira in alarm. "Wh-What?"

"Well, Winterbourne—that's a very prestigious school." Moira studied her nails. "So you're a chichi prep-school brat, eh?"

"Chi . . . what?" Chloe bit her lip. *What did I say wrong?*

Moira lowered her nail file and gave Chloe a snidely incredulous stare. "Come on. Winterbourne? Connecticut? Is your dad, like, a *Fortune* centerfold or what?"

Chloe wanted to sink through the floorboards and die. "No, not at all," she choked through the obstruction in her throat. "I went to Winterbourne on . . . scholarship."

"Reeeally," Moira said again, arching an eyebrow.

Chloe nodded. Her face was burning hot. "I got a lot of, um, financial aid."

Moira nodded. "I see." She tapped her teeth with a newly sharpened fingernail. "Hey, are those real pearls?"

38

Chloe's eyes followed Moira's and fell on the pile of toiletries and trinkets she'd dumped out on her bed. The strand of pearls was tangled up with some plastic beads and a dime-store polyester scarf. Her stomach lurched. *Mom, I could kill you!* she cursed silently.

"Did you get those pearls on scholarship, Chloe?" Moira asked.

Chloe swallowed hard. The lump in her throat was welling up to the size of an orange. She could feel Moira watching her, but for a long moment she was unable to speak.

"They were . . . in the family," she said finally. "You know, I . . . I think I'll finish unpacking later. I feel like checking out the campus a little."

Chloe stumbled out into the hallway, her vision blurred with tears. She felt like kicking herself. God, she was a complete idiot. Moira must think she was immature even by freshman standards.

Well, how was she supposed to know? Chloe asked herself, hugging her arms to her chest. So she'd gone to prep school. What was the big deal? Lots of people went to prep school. It wasn't like she was such an aberration.

What she was, Chloe knew, was in over her head.

"Wait till you see what I'm making!" Todd said over his shoulder.

Dana leaned openmouthed in the kitchen doorway. Todd stood at the stove, wrestling with two pans, both of which were billowing black smoke. "Dinner will be ready in like five minutes."

The entire surface of the counter was littered with broken eggshells and potato peelings. Flour was sprinkled everywhere. A brown, syrupy substance was dripping from the counter and forming a sticky pool on the linoleum floor.

"Todd, what *is* all this?" she finally managed to choke out. "Did we have an earthquake or something?"

"I'm making dinner!" Todd exclaimed in an offended voice. "As a gesture of gratitude to you and your housemates for letting me stay here."

Dana squelched the impulse to offer her

prediction as to how Todd's "gesture" would be interpreted. "That's . . . sweet," she said instead.

"Look, I'm making potatoes au gratin." He gestured at a cast-iron skillet containing an unrecognizable crusty mush.

"You really didn't have to do this," Dana said.

"Of course I did. This is training for when we have real lives, not just dumb college stuff." Todd gave Dana a kiss on the cheek. "When you're a famous cellist and I'm your doting husband, I'd better have dinner ready and waiting for you."

Dana wiped off the dusting of flour Todd's kiss had left on her face. "I thought you were going to be busy with the NBA."

"I'm talking about the *off*-season. Ooh! I almost forgot the dessert." He lifted the lid off a saucepan, revealing a brown substance that seemed to have become one with the pan. "Voilà, *le* chocolate pudding."

"Uh, you might want to lower the heat a little," Dana suggested, twisting her hands together. All the kitchen equipment belonged to Joyce, who was tyrannical about cleanliness.

"And check out the pièce de résistance—spinach quiche." Todd opened the oven door with a flourish. A wall of smoke poured forth. He waved a pot holder to clear the air and peered inside. "Uh-oh."

"What, uh-oh?" Dana stared in dismay into the oven. Eggy yellow liquid had leaked from a

42

bubbling pie tin and was splattered all over the oven in various stages of charredness. The pie crust itself looked as if it were composed of crushed charcoal.

Todd turned to Dana. "But I followed the recipe exactly," he said.

Dana's heart melted at the sight of Todd's crestfallen expression. She burst out laughing and threw her arms around his neck. "You are too adorable. You know, you'll make somebody a good little wife someday."

Todd groaned, but he was grinning too. "If the Board of Health doesn't condemn me first."

Just as their lips brushed together, the smoke alarm went off, sending shrill peals through the kitchen. Dana and Todd broke apart, bursting into laughter at the same time. While Dana frantically waved her arms under the detector, Todd ran to the kitchen window and hoisted it open.

"What is going *on* in here?" Joyce appeared in the doorway. "Is it too much to ask for some peace and—*oh my God!*"

Dana winced as her housemate's eyes grew wide. "Don't worry—we'll clean everything up," she shouted over the alarm.

But Joyce was already at the stove, staring with horror at the caked-on mess Todd had made of her pans. "You can't clean these!" she wailed. "They're all ruined! Do you have any idea how much nice cookware like this costs?"

The siren squeals of the alarm finally subsided. Todd let out his breath and ran his hand through his hair. "I'm really sorry, Joyce—it was all my fault. I'll replace everything for you, I promise."

Joyce whirled and glared daggers at Todd. "I should have known this was *your* doing since it smells like something died in here!"

"What's *that* supposed to mean?" Todd asked. Dana's stomach twisted. She had a very bad feeling about where this was headed.

"It means everything you touch turns to *gross*," Joyce declared, jabbing an accusing finger at Todd. "Our whole apartment's been a sty since you and your sweat socks moved in, and now the kitchen's a total disaster area. Don't you have *any* consideration for the people around you?"

Dana glanced at Todd. His teeth were clamped on his lower lip; she could tell how hard he was trying to keep it together. She put a conciliatory hand on her housemate's arm. "Todd was just trying to make a big dinner," she explained, "to show everybody his appreciation for letting him stay here."

"Oh, really." Joyce shrugged her arm free of Dana's grasp. Her eyes, trained on Todd, were narrowed into glinting shards of white. "Well, Todd, if you *really* want to show us your appreciation, you could think about having us over for dinner at your *own* place."

* * *

44

"So our first priority, obviously, is getting the electricity turned on." Elizabeth leaned closer to the coffee table, where a row of candles flickered, and made a note on her pad. "I can take care of that tomorrow morning."

Neil, on the couch next to Elizabeth, swallowed a bite of pepperoni pizza. "I dunno—I think the mood lighting's kind of nice."

"It is sorta romantic." Jessica, sprawled on the living-room floor, glanced up at Neil a little wistfully. In the soft candlelight his gorgeous face seemed to glow. Jessica sighed and took a bite of pizza. She was forced to remind herself for the millionth time that she had zero chance with Neil.

"Seriously, you guys." Elizabeth tapped her pad with her pencil, reminding Jessica of her second-grade teacher. "We have a million things to do tomorrow."

"Do we have to talk about them now?" Jessica sighed again. She was exhausted, and every muscle in her body ached. "We've all been running around stressed out all day. Can't we take a little breather while we eat?"

"Sorry, Jess, but we can't just blow this stuff off," Elizabeth replied. "Between registering for classes and interviewing roommates, we're not going to have much time tomorrow. Okay, the next thing is the hot water. . . ."

Jessica rolled her eyes, tuning out her twin's control-freak diatribe. It was so Elizabeth to be making type-A lists right now, when Jessica could barely absorb being here. *Living* here. It was so surreal to be shrouded in darkness at sundown, to order pizza from the corner pay phone, to root around in boxes for all her worldly possessions.

Jessica took another bite of pizza. The thought of getting up to register for classes tomorrow was overwhelming. All she wanted was to curl up in bed and sleep for days . . . if only she knew where she was sleeping.

"Jess? *Hello?*"

"What?" Jessica looked up and saw that Elizabeth's pencil was poised expectantly over her pad.

"I *said*, do you want to take care of getting the phone turned on? I'm surprised you're not showing symptoms of withdrawal as it is."

"Very funny." Jessica made a face at her sister. Sometimes Elizabeth seemed to take the attitude that only *she* had grown up, while Jessica had magically remained fourteen years old. "Fine, I'll deal with the phone. But only if we can discuss *my* number-one priority."

"Which is?" Neil asked.

"Picking bedrooms." Jessica tossed a pizza-crust remnant onto her paper plate. "I'm totally wiped, and I want to move my bed before my legs collapse under me."

Elizabeth bit her lip, suddenly looking more anxious than in charge. "Well, how are we going to decide?"

"Let's just discuss why we think we deserve the room we want," Jessica suggested. "For example, maybe certain people, such as myself, need more closet space than others."

"Nice try, Jess," Elizabeth responded. "If anything, *I* should get the big closet since *certain people such as yourself* are always going through my stuff."

"It was worth a shot," Jessica muttered, shredding a paper napkin in frustration. She was getting sick of Elizabeth's constant superior attitude. Did every decision-making process in this house have to involve making Jessica feel inferior?

"Listen, there's only one fair way to decide." Neil reached for the bag of garlic straws that had come with the pizza. "We should just draw straws. Whoever gets the longest gets first pick."

Elizabeth looked horrified. "You mean leave it to *chance?*" she asked. "But this is a big decision— it'll affect a whole year of our lives!"

"Yeah, well, *somebody* has to spend a year in a lousy room," Neil said matter-of-factly. "At least the fourth person will get stuck with the worst one. So, what do you say?"

Jessica hesitated, glancing sideways at her sister. Elizabeth opened her mouth, then closed it, as if she were about to make an objection but couldn't come up with one. Jessica couldn't help sharing her sister's apprehension, but she wasn't in the mood to take Elizabeth's side at the moment. And besides, she was stumped too.

"Well, it's okay with me," Jessica said finally. "Let's just get this over with so I can get some sleep."

She and Neil turned expectantly to Elizabeth, who shrugged. "I guess it's the only way."

"All right, then." Neil ripped a piece off one garlic straw and popped it into his mouth. "Let's do it."

"And remember that time you made an eleventh-hour comeback against USC?" Lance asked, setting down his pint of beer on the bar. "I never saw anybody catch a pass like that in my life. That was just sick, man."

"Oh, yeah . . . that *was* a great game," Tom agreed, sipping his beer. "I haven't thought about that in forever."

"I can still see the whole play in slow motion, just like a movie." Lance waved his arm toward the case of jerseys and pennants mounted on the wall of the off-campus sports bar. "Your number should be up there, Watts. That one play alone made you a legend."

Tom lifted his mug to his lips, hiding his embarrassed grin. "C'mon. Anybody could have caught that pass. I was just in the right place at the right time."

"Are you kidding?" Lance sputtered, slamming his palm down on the bar. "You must've been fifty yards away from anyone else on the field. You were in the end zone before USC knew what hit 'em." He clinked his mug against Tom's. "You're the man, dude."

Tom downed the last of his beer, not knowing what to say. The constant ego boosts Lance was feeding him were totally above and beyond. But totally appreciated. Even though they didn't have much in common, Tom was starting to consider Lance a real friend, not just an acquaintance from his past.

"Am I seeing things?" A booming voice behind him startled Tom. He turned around; it took him a few seconds to place the two guys. Tony Darello and Duke Statler, two guys he'd met on the team as a freshman.

"Wildman, is it really you?" Tony went on. "No *way,* man! I haven't seen you in years!"

"How's it going, man?" Duke clapped Tom on the shoulder as Tony greeted Lance. "Hey, how come you never hang out with us anymore?"

"I—I dunno," Tom stammered, a little overcome. "It's good to see you guys."

"You too, man. It's been too long." Tony hooked his arm around Tom's neck. "The team hasn't been the same since you left."

"Yeah, we still talk about some of those crazy plays you made," Duke agreed. "Dude, you're a legend."

That word again—*legend.* Did anyone actually still think of him that way?

49

"You're gonna turn me into a conceited jerk," Tom said, trying to play it off. It was no wonder he'd been such a superficial fool when he'd been at the center of all this attention 24/7.

"Hey, we wouldn't give you props if you didn't deserve 'em." Lance clapped Tom on the back.

"For real," Tony agreed. "I wish our QB now would take a few pointers from you—maybe we wouldn't have sucked up the AstroTurf last season."

"Would you believe two for sixteen?" Lance shook his head disgustedly. "I swear, you should see this guy. His middle name is *fumble*. Next to you, he looks like he belongs in peewee football."

"Hey, can I get you another round, Wildman?" Tony asked, gesturing at Tom's empty mug. "We've got some serious catching up to do, and if we're going to relive last season, I definitely need a drink."

"Amen to that." Duke groaned, pulling up the stool next to Tom's.

"Thanks, man, that'd be cool." Tom grinned at Tony, adding, "But I've got the next round." He wasn't going to delude himself by letting these guys give him the star treatment. He'd abandoned his superjock life so long ago—it would be a little pathetic to pretend he was still Wildman Watts, big-time football hero.

But for tonight, at least, it would be very, very cool.

50

*   *   *

"*Yes!*" Jessica whooped, raising the unbroken garlic straw over her head. "Walk-in closet, you are mine!" She let out a sigh that sounded to Elizabeth more like pure smugness than relief.

"You don't have to rub it in," Elizabeth muttered, slumping against the couch. She took a dispirited bite of the shortest stub of garlic straw, in her hand.

"Oh, but it's so much fun." Jessica clamped the straw between her teeth. "Okay, Neil, your turn to pick."

"I'm all over that other second-floor room," Neil said. "But Jess, I'm setting some very clear boundaries. Just because we're sharing a bathroom does not mean my toiletries become your toiletries."

"Ha!" Elizabeth said. "I'd lock up your stuff if I were you, Neil."

"I'll ignore that since I know you're bitter, Liz," Jessica said. "So, what's it going to be? Attic or kitchen? It's really a matter of whether you'd prefer your clothes to smell like mothballs or meatballs."

Elizabeth shot Jess the look that told her to watch it or else. "You know," Neil cut in, "the attic's actually really big." Neil leaned his face over one of the candles, shrouding his eyes in shadow, and adopted a deep, ominous voice. "But of course, it might be . . . haunted."

"Thanks for pointing that out." Elizabeth

chewed the inside of her lip as she contemplated the options. Her picture of sophomore year had definitely not included living like the Phantom of the Opera, skulking around in the dusty attic room with its low, sloping ceiling. On the other hand, taking the room next to the kitchen meant trying to study while listening to Jessica bang pots and pans together on the other side of the wall.

"I guess I'll take the attic," she said, managing a smile. "Maybe living like a starving author in a garret will inspire me in my writing. It'll be romantic and picturesque." At least, that was what she would tell herself when she was hobbling around her sloped room, practically doubled over.

"Way to turn lemons into lemonade, Liz," Jessica said. She uncurled her legs and stretched herself up off the floor. "Well, now that that's settled, I'm going to bed. Hopefully I'll dream about showering and using the phone."

"Wait a second." Neil rapped his knuckles on the glass-top coffee table that had graced the Wakefield living room in the seventies. "First I want to bring up *my* top priority. I don't know about you two, but I'm going to be starving for real if we don't find somebody for that downstairs room."

Elizabeth felt like groaning. She could handle having a lot to do, but it was so nerve-racking that everything really did have to get done *right away*. She'd looked forward to living off campus as a way to let loose a little, and now it just seemed like a constant source of stress. If anything, Elizabeth was wound up even tighter than usual.

"Well, we have those appointments for tomorrow," she said, picking up the pad where she'd printed her to-do list. "And once we have a phone number, we can put up flyers."

Jessica was hovering at the foot of the staircase. "What appointments?"

"I told you—the ones I set up while I was crashing at my friend Stan's place," Neil reminded her. "We're meeting with four people—mostly friends of friends. The first one's tomorrow at two-thirty."

Elizabeth squinted at her to-do list, mentally calculating. There was no way she'd be able to get registering out of the way early, like she'd planned. She hadn't even decided for sure on her schedule, and she'd be too busy running around tomorrow to go over the course catalog thoroughly. More stress—what if she got shut out of her journalism seminar?

"I'll be there," Jessica said. "Oh—so are you guys gonna help me move my bed into my great room?"

Perfect, Elizabeth thought. The last thing they had to do tonight involved serious manual labor. "Then my bed, Jess, *right?*"

"And then mine," Neil added.

"Of course," Jessica responded. "Did you

53

really think I'd get you guys to help me and then just blow you off by falling fast asleep?"

Elizabeth and Neil turned to each other and smiled.

"Here's me and Kendrick at the junior prom, and here's me and Kendrick at the senior prom." Shondra Valance held up a silver-framed and a gold-framed picture, both formal portrait shots of herself and a tall, geekily cute boy. "Here we are white-water rafting, and this one was taken last Christmas at his mom's house. Doesn't he look adorable in that sweater? I knitted it for him." Shondra flipped a lock of shiny black hair off her shoulder and giggled.

"You two make a great couple," Nina said, nodding. Her suite mate had been playing boyfriend show-and-tell since she arrived two hours ago. The floor of the suite's common room was scattered with snapshots and other Kendrick memorabilia. Shondra seemed nice, and she was outgoing, but Nina wasn't in the mood to be re-galed with mushy high-school-sweetheart stories.

"Thanks! Do you really think so?" Shondra hugged the pictures to her chest and sighed dreamily. Sitting cross-legged on the floor with her white sundress spread around her, she looked to Nina like a priestess performing some ritual of worship to Kendrick. "You know, I truly believe everybody has a soul mate, and Kendrick is mine."

"That's great," Nina said. She crouched over the open cardboard box on the floor and started extracting the cassettes inside. Hopefully Shondra would catch the hint that sharing time was over. If this gush fest went on much longer, Nina was going to puke all over the prom photos.

"I know what you're thinking." Giggling again, Shondra reached over and lightly punched Nina's arm. "Don't worry—he's two thousand miles away, so he won't be visiting me all that often. And when he does, we'll keep the noise down."

How considerate of you, Nina thought, stacking her tapes beside the portable stereo atop her minifridge. "Long distance," she replied instead. "That must be tough." She turned to another cardboard box.

Shondra shrugged and put the Christmas picture next to Nina's stereo. "It's hell on my phone bills, but our relationship's really strong, so we can deal." She gazed at the picture for a second before turning earnest brown eyes on Nina. "Sorry, I've totally been babbling about myself. What about you, Nina? Do you have a boyfriend?"

Nina stabbed at the box's masking-taped seam with her Swiss army knife. She dragged the knife through the tape and unfolded the flaps before responding. "I'm . . . really focused on my work right now. Too busy for men."

"Awww, you've gotta have fun *some*time!" Shondra wiped dust off the prom picture with the hem of her sundress. "Come on, you're pretty and nice, and you must be supersmart if you really read all those books." She gestured toward the thick physics volumes Nina had stacked in the built-in bookcase. "I bet there are tons of guys dying to go out with you."

Nina didn't respond. She was staring at the face that had greeted her when she opened the box. Bryan's face—smiling broadly up at Nina through the silver frame he'd given her on their one-month anniversary. His brown eyes shone with an expression she remembered from those first magical weeks together. It was a look of love mixed with wonder, as if he still couldn't believe they'd really found each other.

Nina felt her chest tightening, a lump welling in her throat. She rifled through the box, past more pictures she couldn't even look at. Below them was a book of poetry Bryan had given her, a bundle of his love letters, and a cheesy but beloved little teddy bear he'd won for her at a carnival. Everything she had to show for her entire relationship with Bryan was packed into this two-foot-square box. Nina couldn't imagine anything more depressing.

"Nina?" Shondra was saying. "Are you okay? Did I say something wrong?"

"Yeah, I'm fine." Nina stood up and hefted the

box into her arms. "Excuse me for a minute. I'm just going to get rid of some old junk."

As she marched down the hall, Nina realized her eyes were stinging. Was it ever going to stop? These constant reminders of Bryan were torture.

When classes started, she'd have a distraction, Nina consoled herself, blinking back tears. She'd be so busy, she wouldn't have time to obsess about Bryan.

But it was cold comfort. She could throw herself into her course work, but she couldn't shut out her dorm mates' questions . . . or her own sense of emptiness, of drifting without an anchor. In spite of herself Nina felt a tear snake down her cheek.

She reached the trash chute, dropped the box on the floor, and wiped the tear away with her sweatshirt sleeve. She'd get him out of her mind somehow, she vowed, drawing a shaky breath.

Nina dumped out the contents of the box down the chute and headed back to her room, feeling leaden and numb. The school year hadn't even started, and already she was counting the days until it was over.

Chapter Four

"So, Jessica, what can I do for you?" Professor Wyckoff pushed a pair of delicate, silver-framed glasses past the bridge of her nose.

Jessica lifted just slightly off her chair to hand her registration forms across her adviser's desk. "Well, I basically just need approval on most of my classes. But there are a couple I can't decide between. I'm sort of hoping to . . . try something different this year." She tucked her short, stretchy skirt carefully underneath her as she sat back down. For some reason, it seemed important to make a good impression, even though she'd had the same adviser last year.

The professor nodded, scanning the papers. "That's a smart move. I like to see undergraduates broadening their horizons."

"Thanks." Jessica straightened her spine. Maybe it wasn't too late to start taking school more seriously. She was doing pretty well so far. It was impressive in itself that she had gotten up bright and early on a Monday to get her classes approved. Well, okay, it *was* two o'clock by the time she got to campus, but it was only the first day of registration. Definitely not Jessica's usual last-minute schedule.

She adopted her most adult tone. "My main issue is, do I want to take a film course or something more along the lines of art history?"

Professor Wyckoff nodded. "Well, the film department and the art-history department are both great, so it really depends on what makes more sense for your major." She frowned at Jessica's form. "I see you left that field blank. Have you thought about what you're going to major in, Jessica?"

"Major?" Jessica laced her fingers together in her lap and squeezed them into a white-knuckled fist. "Actually, I was kind of, uh, keeping my options open."

Professor Wyckoff set the form down on her desk and looked at Jessica. "You do realize that this is the semester you have to declare."

"Oh, of course. I was just, um, kidding." Jessica laughed nervously. The truth was, she'd totally spaced about the whole declaring-a-major issue. When Professor Wyckoff brought it up last fall, sophomore year had seemed as distant a future as hovercrafts and superhumans with hugely inflated brains. It hadn't mattered that she had no clue what she wanted to do with her life.

Jessica had always been the type of person who rushed headlong into new projects—and veered off course just as suddenly. But a major was the first step in a long, unwavering path. If she picked wrong, she could end up bored and miserable for the rest of her college career . . . not to mention her *real* career, although *that* seemed even further off than the big-head people.

Professor Wyckoff cleared her throat, snapping Jessica out of a disturbing vision of herself in a plastic visor and an apron that read: Ask Me About Our Chili Special. "I know that this can be a daunting decision, but it's not like your life is set in stone once you choose your undergrad major."

"It's just that I don't know exactly what I want to do yet," Jessica confessed, twisting her hands in her lap.

She was ashamed to tell the whole truth—that she'd barely even given it a thought. Her visions of the future had always been pipe dreams—fantasies of posing for *Vogue* or thanking the Academy. Now she wanted something real, something she could really make happen . . . and somehow that seemed even more unlikely. Elizabeth had her writing and her lifetime of straight A's. What did Jessica have?

Her adviser smiled. "Believe me, Jessica, you're not the first student who's broken out into a cold sweat when I say the *M* word, and you won't be the last. Listen, why don't we go over your transcript from last year and see what you concentrated on? Often students rack up credits that count toward a certain major just by gravitating toward their interests."

"Okay," Jessica agreed, although she doubted that her record would speak well for her. All the personal turmoil she'd gone through last year hadn't exactly done wonders for her GPA.

Professor Wyckoff consulted Jessica's form, then turned to her computer and made a few keystrokes. Her forehead creased as she scanned the screen. "Huh," she said. She typed in something else and reclined in her desk chair, two fingertips pressed against her lips. "This is strange."

"What's strange? What do you mean?" Jessica chewed her lip and squirmed in her chair. Were her grades that appalling?

"Well, I pulled up your record, but it doesn't list you as an active student," Professor Wyckoff explained. "According to the system, you're not enrolled."

"*What?*" Jessica gasped. "That must be a mistake!"

"I'll double-check." Professor Wyckoff punched some more keys, waited for a second, then shook her head. "I'm sorry, Jessica, but apparently you're not enrolled in SVU for the fall semester."

"But how . . . why . . . how could that happen?"

The professor spread out her hands. "I have no idea, Jessica. That's really a matter for the registrar's office."

Jessica shot up out of her seat and snatched her registration forms off her adviser's desk. She realized her legs were shaking. "I'm sorry, but I have to go to the registrar and take care of this," she said a little breathlessly. "Before I start agonizing over any life-altering decisions, I'd like to make sure I'm actually a student here."

"Have you seen Jessica?" Neil stomped into the kitchen to find Elizabeth perched on a stool at the counter, reading a course catalog.

Elizabeth looked startled. "She went out about an hour ago." She glanced at her watch and groaned. "I can't believe it's two-thirty already."

"Exactly my point," Neil said. "Our first appointment's going to show up any second. Where the hell is she? She promised to be here!"

"I'm sure she'll be back soon," Elizabeth said, flipping a page in the catalog.

"Well, did you remind her about the interviews when she left?" Neil demanded.

"It hadn't occurred to me to remind her," she responded a little defensively. "I mean, we did have a whole conversation about it last night. It was her responsibility to remember." She slapped the catalog shut.

Neil leaned against the counter, his temples throbbing, and silently counted to ten once again. It figured that Elizabeth would choose the most inopportune moment to stop her big-sister-little-sister nagging.

He exhaled deeply. It wasn't Elizabeth's fault, but at times like these it was hard not to think of the twins as one entity—with unlimited rent money. Sometimes Neil wondered if they even grasped the fact that if he ran out of money, he would be out on the street.

The front doorbell rang. Elizabeth looked at Neil in alarm. "Should we just go ahead without Jess?"

Neil sighed. "What choice do we have?" He headed toward the living room. "All I can say is, if we like this guy, he's moving in, and Jessica doesn't get to say a word about it."

"But that's not really fair," Elizabeth protested, following him. "We should make sure everyone gets along if we're all going to live together."

"This isn't about making friends—it's about being able to afford a roof over our heads," Neil growled. "But we'll talk about it later." He plastered on a big, friendly smile and flung open the door. "Hi, you must be . . ."

Neil trailed off, his smile draining. Slouched in the doorway was an all-black-leather-clad guy who looked like a cross between Edward Scissorhands and something out of *Hellraiser*. Silver rings were threaded through his eyebrows, nose, and upper lip, and a sharp-looking spike protruded from his chin. His face was dusted with sheet-white makeup; his hair was jet black and gelled straight up, and, Neil noticed with revulsion, his earlobes were stretched almost to his chin by clear plastic plugs that fitted where earrings would be.

". . . Damian Cross," Neil finished, recovering his composure. He reminded himself that he didn't believe in judging people by appearances. At least the guy knew how to accessorize. "I'm Neil Martin, and this is Elizabeth Wakefield."

"Uh-huh," Damian said, his face expressionless. Maybe smiling would stretch his piercings, Neil thought.

"Nice to meet you. Come on in." Neil ushered Damian inside and sat down beside him on the couch.

Elizabeth lowered herself onto the edge of an armchair opposite them. A small, fake, nervous smile seemed frozen on her face.

Neil waited a minute for Damian to volunteer something—anything—then cleared his throat. "So, what year are you?"

"Grad student." When Damian opened his mouth, Neil caught a flash of a silver tongue stud. "First year."

Elizabeth's frozen smile melted just a little. "What are you studying?"

"Philosophy." Apparently exhausted by that

conversational tour de force, Damian lapsed into silence, making eye contact with some point in the distance.

"So, would you like to see the room?" Elizabeth offered.

Damian inclined his head in what Neil figured was a yes.

"Well, then," Elizabeth said, practically bolting out of her chair. "Right this way." Damian stood, and Elizabeth led the way through the kitchen. "It is kind of small," she called over her shoulder. She opened the door to the narrow room and switched on the light. "Here it is."

Damian nodded. "It's not that small. I could build some shelves for my four track."

"Four track?" Neil echoed, hoping that didn't mean what he thought it meant.

"Yeah, for recording music?" For the first time Damian began to look animated. "I'm really into old-school industrial music. You know, like Skinny Puppy, Nine Inch Nails? I'm in this industrial band called Live Alien Circuits—well, actually, I'm the only one in the band, but I record under that name. You should check us . . . uh, me, out."

Neil didn't have to glance at Elizabeth to guess her reaction . . . but he did anyway, just for fun. She was looking at Damian as though he had five heads. Neil suppressed a smile. He wasn't exactly clicking with Damian himself, but Elizabeth was clearly so out of her element, it was absurd.

He decided it was time to cut their losses.

"Well, it was nice meeting you." Neil stuck out his hand to Damian and instantly felt Elizabeth relax beside him.

"Phone for you." Moira held out the receiver to Chloe. "It's your mommy."

Chloe felt her arms prickle into goose bumps. She grabbed the phone and sat down on her bed, her back to Moira. "Mom? What's up? How did you get this number?"

"Oh, I made a few calls to the school," Lillian Murphy said. That was her answer to everything— making a few calls. Chloe put her palm to her forehead and squeezed her eyes shut, silently cursing her mother. Chloe had planned to spend a few days settling in, then call home with her number. But of course, she should have known her parents wouldn't let her have a moment to herself.

"Anyway, Chlo, your dad and I have been talking," Mrs. Murphy went on. "We just can't stand the thought of you sleeping on a moldy old mattress in some roach-infested dorm room. So we made a couple of calls and got you first look at a penthouse apartment just off campus. It's got all the amenities—doorman, laundry, all-new furnishings. . . ."

"Mom, we've had this discussion a million times," Chloe said in a low voice. "How many times do I have to tell you? I'm fine." She turned slightly to dart a wary glance at Moira, who was humming to herself as she polished her toenails. The last thing Chloe wanted was for her roommate to pick up on what her mom was saying.

"Well," her mother went on, "I just assumed that once you saw what kind of cramped quarters you're stuck in, you'd reconsider. Really, Chloe, you should see this place. The management faxed us some pictures, and—"

"I'm *fine*, Mom," Chloe repeated. "Could you just trust me on this?"

There was an exasperated sigh on the other end of the line. "I just can't stand to think of you living in such substandard conditions. Why don't you let us help—"

"Because I don't need your help!" Chloe snapped, then cringed when she realized how loudly. Although her back was to Moira, Chloe could practically sense her roommate's eavesdropping antennae going up. She cupped her hand around the mouthpiece and lowered her voice. "I want to start doing things for myself. Which reminds me, Mom—I can't believe you hid those clothes in my bag. You had *no* right to do that! I'm perfectly capable of packing my *own* luggage."

"Well, I saw what you laid out for yourself, sweetie, and I just knew you wouldn't be able to get by on those things," her mother said. "I mean, how can you pledge Theta in those ratty, disgusting T-shirts? You want to make an impression, don't you?"

Yes, but not your *kind of impression,* Chloe wanted to say. She gripped the mouthpiece tighter. "Maybe I don't want to rush Theta or any sorority. Maybe I just want to experience school on my own for a while, not as . . . part of some society."

"But you *are* part of a society, dear," Mrs. Murphy said in the patient voice she used with small children and servants. "You represent our family, and since I was a Theta, you represent *me* specifically at SVU. It would be nice if you put a *little* thought into the kind of impression you project."

Chloe felt her insides twist. "Mom, this is *my* life, okay? Not the entire family's!" She was fighting to keep her voice down, acutely aware of Moira listening even though she couldn't halt the flow of words. "I'm not your spoiled little girl anymore! Can't you just let me live my own life, like a normal person?"

Mrs. Murphy sucked in her breath so sharply that Chloe half expected her ear to be pulled through the receiver. "Fine. Pardon me for trying to make your life easier. It won't happen again."

Chloe instantly felt guilty and sorry. "Mom, I know you were just trying to—"

"Never mind." Mrs. Murphy's tone was clipped. "We'll talk about this later. Your father and I have a dinner engagement, and I have to go get dressed."

"Love you," Chloe said, but her mother had already hung up the phone. She replaced the receiver and realized that she was shaking. Everything she'd said to her mother was what she'd been dying to say for months, maybe years. She just hadn't known it would feel so awful.

Jessica was panting as she jogged up the stairs that led into the registrar's office. She pushed through the front doors and slowed to a walk, her heavy breaths echoing across the marble lobby. She wasn't sure whether the nauseous sensation in the pit of her stomach was from tearing across campus right after a large iced mocchacino or from sheer terror that she wasn't enrolled. If she wasn't enrolled, then she wasn't really a sophomore. If she wasn't a sophomore, then she couldn't make her fresh start. If she—

Chill out! Jessica told herself. *Just go take care of it!*

Signs pointed her down a long corridor. Jessica broke into a sprint again, unable to calm the adrenaline-producing panic. After several twists and turns, she found herself in the main registrar's office, a large room with a row of five bank-teller-like windows at the back. The mazelike line of students that wound through the room was longer than some Jessica had seen at amusement parks. She took her place at the end of the line, her breath gradually slowing.

As the herd of students inched excruciatingly forward, Jessica felt like she might jump out of her own skin with frustration. It was so unfair. Her first day of trying to be more adult, of taking control of her own life—and *this* had to happen. She kept telling herself it must be some computer glitch, some insignificant error that could be cleared up by pressing a few buttons. But with every agonizing minute she spent in line, Jessica's sense of dread coiled a little tighter in her stomach. What would she do if she couldn't get reinstated as a student? She couldn't even begin to process that possibility.

It took at least an hour for Jessica to wind her way to the front of the line. She made a beeline for the first open window and exhaled a rushing stream of words. "Hi,mynameisJessicaWakefieldandI—"

"ID number?" the middle-aged woman behind the glass asked in the most bored voice Jessica had ever heard.

Jessica fished her student ID out of her purse and slid it through the hollowed slot in the window ledge. "Anyway, my adviser just told me I'm not enrolled for the fall semester, and I don't understand it. I mean, I sent in all my . . ."

She trailed off, unsure if the clerk was paying

71

attention to her at all. The woman was alternately scrutinizing Jessica's ID and pecking computer keys at a numbingly slow pace. Jessica resisted the urge to pound frantically on the Plexiglas.

"Excuse me?" Jessica said instead. "Are you looking at my record? What does it say?"

The woman blinked at her monitor for what seemed like five minutes. "Wakefield, Elizabeth?" she asked finally, without looking up.

Jessica clenched her hands into fists. "No, *Jessica!*"

The clerk turned away from her monitor and fixed Jessica with a pointed glare. "There's no need to shout," she said, before slowly swiveling her head back toward the screen. "Wakefield, Jessica . . . yes."

"Yes, what?"

"Yes, you're not enrolled."

Jessica clapped her hands over her face. This wasn't happening. This was a bad dream. Any minute she'd wake up in her gorgeous new room, surrounded by half-unpacked boxes. She forced herself to take a deep breath. "Can you please tell me *why* I'm not enrolled?"

The woman shrugged. "Doesn't say. It's probably a nonpayment issue."

"But my parents mailed the check like a month ago!" Jessica wailed.

"Sorry, I can't help you." The clerk slid Jessica's ID back through the window. "That's not our department. You have to see the bursar for that."

Jessica wanted to scream, but instead she grabbed her ID card and dashed out of the office. Campus was a blur at the edges of her vision as she hurried toward the bursar's office. "Unbelievable," she muttered to herself. "Unreal." This whole situation was getting more nightmarish by the minute. What a wretched way to kick off sophomore year.

The line at the bursar's office was only slightly shorter than the one at the registrar's. As she waited, Jessica gnawed her cuticles, shifted her weight around, rocked back and forth on her heels, and twirled her hair around her index finger. *It'll be over soon,* she told herself again and again. *They'll straighten everything out—they have to.*

Finally she reached the front of the line and gave the balding man behind the counter her name and ID number. "It says I'm not enrolled, but I know I'm all paid up," she explained. "There's been some mistake."

The man glanced up from his monitor and smiled. "I'm sorry, but this does list your enrollment in SVU as being on hold. We *have* received your parental contribution for the semester, but we have no record of your student loan having come through. It looks like that's the problem."

"So what do I do?" Jessica asked.

"You'll have to consult a loan officer. They're located at the financial-aid office."

"*Another* office?" Jessica moaned, and sprinted out of the bursar's, then stopped in her tracks, slapped her forehead, and sprinted right back in.

"Can anyone *please* tell me how to get to the financial-aid office?" she wailed, hopping on one foot to relieve the pressure of the gigantic blister forming on the other.

"I only want to take about twelve credits this semester," Lance explained through a mouthful of cheeseburger. "So I need one more four-credit class, and then I'm set."

"What do you think about twentieth-century political science?" Across the diner booth Tom lowered his course catalog to the table and sucked a thick sip of vanilla milk shake through his straw. "That might even count toward your history major."

Lance munched a clump of chili cheese fries before responding. "Well, I guess I could find out what the course requirements are. I'm not taking any classes where they make you write more than two papers."

"How do you . . . oh, right." Tom recalled how he used to check with his adviser to get the scoop on exactly what his semester's workload would be. Student athletes were encouraged to make sure their course loads were cushy enough to accommodate a grueling practice schedule.

"If my average dips below a C, I'm off the team," Lance said, wiping a smear of mustard from his chin. "So I like to cut myself some slack, y'know? Better to aim low and exceed expectations than the other way around, I always say."

"Can't argue with that." Tom scanned his own list of courses as he dragged on his milk shake. So far he had seventeen credits, ten of which were intensive-journalism seminars. He'd be logging a lot of hours—and that wasn't even counting his work at WSVU, if he decided to take that up again. Well, wasn't that what he should do? Challenge himself, recommit himself to his work?

Lance swabbed a fry in a pool of ketchup. "I mean, football takes a lot out of you. Last season, I was so burnt out that I had to take an incomplete in my medieval-history class. Coach and my adviser took care of the whole thing for me—they were totally cool about it."

"That's awesome." Tom took a bite of his burger and tried to remember if there had ever been a time when he'd let himself slack off. Even when he was on the team, he hadn't fully exploited the opportunity to coast.

"You know, you're lucky," Tom said. "Being an athlete, it's like you have this great support system. You've got people looking out for you and making sure you don't screw up. I kind of miss that."

Lance swallowed a mouthful of chili and stared

at Tom. "Are you serious? Because if you wanted to come back to the team, I know Coach would make it happen like that." He snapped his fingers. "Even if you're a little rusty, I guarantee you could mop up the floor with our first-string QB."

"Oh, I didn't mean . . ." Tom was about to say that he had no intention of going back to the team. But then it occurred to him to wonder what was standing in his way.

"Just think about it," Lance urged. "Man, we'd all be so psyched to have you back."

Tom stared at his list of courses. He stared at the course catalog. It wasn't like he needed to accumulate many more credits. He could afford to be a dumb jock for a while if that would make him happy.

Who knows? he thought. Maybe it would.

Chapter Five

"I can't believe you made me deal with the Prince of Darkness all by myself." Neil groaned, collapsing against the couch. "Maybe if you'd helped at all, together we would have demonstrated enough social skills to make up one whole person."

Elizabeth laughed, even though she did feel a little sheepish about her reaction to Damian. "I'm sorry—I just couldn't think of what to say to him. I kept worrying one of those rings was going to snag on something."

"All those open wounds." Neil shuddered.

Elizabeth frowned as she glanced at her watch. "I can't even believe Jessica hasn't at least called. Not that it's not like her to blow off important stuff, but I would have thought she would start acting more responsibly now that we have our own place."

The doorbell rang, and Neil sighed. "It's your turn to play the good host," he informed Elizabeth, crossing his arms over his chest.

"No problem," Elizabeth said. "After all, this one can't be any weirder than the last guy, right?"

"Famous last words," Neil mumbled as Elizabeth opened the front door.

A thick cloud of gray smoke billowed through the doorway. Elizabeth instantly went into a coughing fit, her eyes watering.

She waved her hands in front of her face until the air cleared to reveal a short, slim girl and a tall, lanky guy. The girl was holding a cigarette stub between two fingers, puffing as if her life depended on it. The guy hovered awkwardly behind her, shoulders bowed, with his hands in his pockets. His unshaven face was partially hidden by greasy hair.

"Hello?" Elizabeth managed to wheeze.

"Hi, I'm Sharon Frye!" the girl exclaimed, sticking out her free hand. Elizabeth shook it, noticing how yellow Sharon's fingertips were. "And this is my boyfriend, Carleton! If I move in, he might stay here some nights—would that be okay? Seriously, you won't even notice him. See how quiet he is? This is really a great place you guys have here!" She stubbed out her cigarette right on the doorstep and lit a fresh one, exhaling tendrils of smoke through her nostrils.

"Thanks," Elizabeth croaked, wondering how

Sharon could smoke so much and still maintain the lung capacity to utter so many words in one breath. "I'm Elizabeth Wakefield."

"Neil Martin," Neil called out from where he sat on the sofa.

"This house is so cute!" Sharon exclaimed, poking her head through the doorway and looking around. "I could really see myself here." She expelled several smoke rings in rapid succession. Elizabeth wrinkled her nose at the smell of tobacco that surrounded the girl. "So can I check out the room?"

"Sure." Elizabeth cleared her throat. Neil was looking back and forth from her to Sharon's cigarette. "But, um, just so you know . . . this is a nonsmoking apartment. So you'd have to smoke outside—"

Elizabeth broke off as Sharon turned around and walked away, Carleton trotting obediently behind. "Thanks anyway," Sharon called over her shoulder before disappearing down the street in a puff of smoke.

"It's about time!" Jessica muttered as she marched up to the first available financial-aid window. Waiting in three monster lines in one day was more than she could stand. Every last nerve in her body was frayed. And choosing today to break in her new strappy sandals had been a *really* bad idea.

79

Just as she reached the window, the clerk slapped a card against the glass. It read: Sorry, We're Closed. Jessica gaped in disbelief.

"Excuse me!" she shouted to the clerk's retreating back. "I've been waiting here for *hours!* You have to help me!"

The woman turned around, and Jessica felt relief flood through her. "All I *have* to do is catch the five-eleven bus," she said. "It's five o'clock—the office is closed. Come back tomorrow."

"Tomorrow?" Jessica shrieked. "I can't wait until tomorrow! You have to help me. You have to! I'm not enrol—"

"Tomorrow." The woman turned her back.

"Wait! Come back!" Jessica realized that tears were spilling down her face. She was actually crying! She hated herself for being such a baby. But she couldn't halt the outburst of all her pent-up frustration. "Don't you understand? They're telling me I'm not even a student, and it's not my fault, and I don't even know *why,* and—"

"Hey . . . hey . . . hey! Relax!" A soft male voice broke through her sobs. Jessica wiped her eyes with the sleeve of her lavender sweater and looked up to see a cute guy smiling at her. He had spiky dark hair, enormous brown eyes, and a neatly trimmed goatee that did nothing to add years to his baby face.

"I don't mind staying late to help you," he said, and Jessica detected the slightest lilt of an accent. "I can't stand to see a beautiful woman cry."

Instantly she took an alarmed mental inventory of what she must look like—face flushed and makeup streaked from crying, hair all flyaway from dashing across campus. Jessica ran a hand through her hair and smiled at the guy through lowered eyes. "That is so sweet of you. God, you must think I'm the biggest baby for freaking out like that."

He waved his hand. "Don't worry about it. The financial-aid office seems to have that effect on people. But I can try to straighten out your problem if it's something relatively simple."

Jessica beamed her brightest smile and fished out her student-ID card.

"Excuse me." Chloe smiled across the dining-hall counter at the hair-netted work-study student who was ladling soup out from a tureen. "Could I have a bowl of French onion, please?"

The girl shot Chloe a resentful glare. "You're supposed to serve yourself—I just bus trays. I'm on my *dinner break*. I do get to eat too, you know."

Chloe cringed and mumbled a flustered apology before sliding her tray down the line. She could live without the soup—she'd go without dinner for a week rather than look that girl in the eye again. God, it was embarrassing that she couldn't even figure out how the cafeteria worked.

Chloe pushed her tray to the end of the counter and glanced from the salad bar to the sandwich counter to the soup tureens. Everyone else was bustling around, serving themselves, as if they were in their own kitchens—even some people who looked familiar from freshman orientation. Why was it so hard for Chloe to figure out what she was doing?

A group of big guys lumbered by, jostling Chloe and nearly knocking the tray out of her hands. She navigated through the swarms of students and took refuge off to the side of the room.

A line of plastic dispensers filled with cereal was set up against the wall. Cereal—that seemed safe. Chloe took a bowl from a stack and placed it under the dispenser. She pulled the lever, and instantly the bowl was buried under an avalanche of cornflakes.

There was a snicker behind her. Chloe felt her face burn but didn't dare turn around.

She leveled off the bowl of cereal and managed to add milk to the bowl without spilling too much. Ignoring the feeling that everyone was staring at her pathetic, milk-soaked tray, Chloe proceeded to the register. She watched carefully as the two people in front of her swiped their meal-plan cards, and Chloe did the same. At least she got that right.

She looked around at the sea of tables, where students sat eating. Laughter and chatter echoed off the high ceilings of the wood-paneled room.

Clutching her tray, Chloe wove her way past table after table of animated faces. Everyone else spilling out into the room seemed to have a destination, a group to join. There were some empty tables toward the back of the room. Chloe slowed her pace, deliberating. Would she look like a huge loser if she sat down by herself?

Maybe she could conveniently "happen" to run into someone she knew and would get invited to sit down. Chloe scanned the room until she spotted a cluster of girls from her dorm—Anoushka Koll, Moira's friend Eva Bedford, and several freshman girls Chloe recognized but didn't know by name.

She headed for their table. As she passed, she slowed her pace and glanced up.

Anoushka caught her eye and smiled, and Eva gave her a little nod of acknowledgment. Then they turned back to each other, deep in conversation.

Chloe's shoulders were slumped as she shuffled to an empty table at the back of the room. She felt completely and conspicuously dweeby sitting down by herself with a tray covered in spilled cereal. Robotically she shoveled spoonfuls of cornflakes into her mouth without tasting them. The faster she ate, the faster she could retreat to her dorm room and try to shake off her overwhelming sense of shame.

Yeah, right, she realized. Like Moira the sophomore would really offer comforting advice. And like Chloe would ever let that witch see her like this.

It was becoming painfully obvious that Chloe wasn't out of place simply because she was a freshman. All the other girls in her class seemed to be adjusting just fine, fitting into cliques. But Chloe didn't fit anywhere at SVU.

"I have plenty of references," Morton Chomsky asserted pleasantly, adding a sheet of paper to the pile on the coffee table. "And all the information for a credit check is right here with these materials, but please let me know ASAP if you need anything else."

Neil exchanged glances with Elizabeth, then turned back to the pudgy, balding man. "Actually, we're not planning on doing credit checks. We're just students—we don't even have credit ratings ourselves yet."

"Oh, just starting out. That's super." Morton blinked through his Coke-bottle lenses and pushed the thick frames back on the bridge of his nose. "FYI, I've got an accounting degree from a two-year college. But all that info is on my applications." He patted the pile of paper as if it were a beloved pet.

FYI? ASAP? Who talked like that? Neil was a little at a loss. Morton seemed like a really nice guy, but he had to be at least forty. Not that there was anything wrong with that, but Neil wondered how psyched Morton would be if they decided to throw a big party or blasted music late at night. And how would Morton react if Neil brought a guy home?

"Well, it was really nice to meet you," Neil said with a smile. "We have a few other people to see, so . . . we'll let you know."

"Thanks for your time." Morton stood up and tugged at his navy blue suit. He extracted a card from his breast pocket and laid it on top of the pile. "Here's my business card—feel free to call my office if you need to touch base."

Elizabeth got up too. "I'll show you to the door."

Neil stretched out on the couch and squeezed his eyes shut. He felt like all the pressure was slowly closing in on him like a vise. It had seemed like such a no-brainer to find a housemate for a great place so close to campus. Deep down he agreed with Elizabeth—it *would* be cool to find someone they clicked with, not just anyone who could pay the rent. But he couldn't afford that luxury. There was nobody he could turn to for a loan to float him until they found the right person.

Elizabeth dropped onto the couch beside him.

"FYI, I don't think I can live with anyone who abbreviates words into letters."

In spite of his worries, Neil grinned. "But just think of all the time he saves talking like that. He must get so much done in a day!"

Elizabeth laughed and groaned at the same time. "I just don't get it. Why is this so hard? Maybe we're being too picky. I mean, it wasn't like we chose the people we were stuck with on the road trip this summer, and we all got along okay."

"Yeah, maybe the trick is that you can't choose the people you end up clicking with," Neil mused. "You, Jess, Sam . . . I never would've ended up getting close to you guys if we hadn't been thrown together like that."

"Some people are harder to get close to than others," she muttered to her lap.

Neil was about to ask what she meant when he realized that he'd mentioned Sam's name.

"You still haven't heard from him, huh?" he asked.

"Who—oh, you mean Sam?" Elizabeth cleared her throat. "Nope—no call, no postcard, nothing." She let out a little laugh. "But that's Sam for you—it's not like I really expected him to keep in touch."

"Yeah, he's a tough guy to pin down." Neil couldn't tell if Elizabeth was more affected by losing touch with Sam than she let on. Over the summer the two of them had really seemed like they were on the verge of something major for a while. But Sam and Elizabeth were like oil and water, so Neil had taken them at their word when they said they'd amicably decided to cut their losses.

Then again, he reflected, sometimes the people who were the most wrong for you were the ones who really got under your skin. That he unfortunately knew from experience.

"Anyway." Elizabeth slapped her palms against her thighs, shattering the silence that had descended over them. "Three down, one to go. What time is the last one getting here again?"

"Five-thirty," Neil murmured, still distracted by the knot in his chest that formed and tightened whenever he thought of Stanford.

Elizabeth glanced at her watch. "Well, it's just about six now. Looks like Jessica's not the only one to blow us off today."

"What?" Neil shook himself back to the present. "Man, it's just one thing after another. At this rate we're never going to get that month of rent back. Which means I pretty much won't eat for the next month."

Elizabeth put a consoling hand on his shoulder. "I'm sure it can't be that bad. Couldn't your parents help you out a little, just till you get settled?"

The knot tightened. He couldn't bring himself

to look at Elizabeth. She had no idea. No idea at all.

For the millionth time he relived the dizzying, punch-in-the-gut feeling of his father's voice cutting through him like a blade: *If that's the lifestyle you've chosen for yourself, don't expect any support from us. . . ."*

"The only person who can help me," Neil said, "is the one who can cough up a month of rent."

"Okay, I think I see what the problem is." Alejandro Morales stroked his goatee thoughtfully as he stared at the monitor. "See, your record doesn't show that we received your loan . . . but your sister, Elizabeth, was credited with *twice* the amount of hers. So I think that whoever processed the payments saw two Wakefields and accidentally processed them into the same file."

Jessica was perched on the desk behind him in the inner sanctum of the financial-aid office. She heaved a deep sigh of relief. "That makes sense. Thank you so much!"

"Let me just double-check." Alejandro swung his wheeled chair over to a filing cabinet and bent his head over a drawer. "Wade, Waggoner . . . Wakefield. Okay." He extracted two folders and flipped through them. "Yes!" He held up a piece of paper triumphantly. "This was in your sister's file, but it has your name on it."

Jessica cheered and clapped. "Alejandro, you're a genius. I can't thank you enough."

"It was my pleasure." Alejandro grinned up at her, revealing an adorable dimple in his chin just above his beard. She was surprised she wasn't flirting like crazy with him. Usually Jessica would launch instantly into autopilot flirt mode, crossing her legs under her and letting her smile turn seductive—especially while a guy was helping her out.

It's because I cared more about getting enrolled than getting a date with a cute guy, Jessica realized, almost stunned.

"Now let me just make these changes in your record." Alejandro turned back to his computer and punched a few keys. "You're lucky that I worked full-time in this office over the summer, or I wouldn't have been able to help you past figuring out the problem." He punched another key. "And there you go! Jessica Wakefield, you are now a first-semester sophomore enrolled at SVU."

Jessica hopped off the desk and onto her feet. "Thank you *sooo* much," she said. "You just totally saved my life. Now all I have to do is declare a major . . . not that that's going to be a picnic."

Alejandro swiveled his chair to look deep into her eyes. "Really? You don't know what you want to major in?"

Jessica shook her head, feeling a little less elated than she had a minute ago. "No clue." She was uncomfortably aware of Alejandro's curious gaze. "Why do you look so surprised?"

Alejandro shrugged. "Well, I know I just met you, but you seem so . . . determined. So full of energy. You seem like the kind of woman who knows what she wants and goes after it." He grinned. "Sorry if that sounded like a line. It wasn't."

Jessica smiled. "Even if it was, I appreciate the vote of confidence. The truth is, I *do* go after what I want—it's just that it changes from minute to minute. Sometimes I think I'll get into film or drama or design or something kind of, I don't know, glamorous." Alejandro was nodding so sincerely that she didn't even feel weird about confessing all this stuff. "Then sometimes I think I should play it safe and do something a little more academic, like English or art history."

"Art history is what *I'm* gonna major in!" Alejandro's eyes lit up. "When I look at art, really look at it, it's like I'm talking to the artist himself— even if he's been dead for a hundred years. Art is so amazing!"

Jessica liked art too, but she'd never felt like she was talking to anyone when she looked at a painting. It would be so cool to feel that passionately about something. Now that she planned to take school seriously, maybe she'd feel that way too, maybe even about art.

"I hope I can get into Professor Strimbaugh's Madness and Modernity seminar," he continued. "All I heard this summer and this week from students coming in this office was how great that class is. You should definitely check it out. I'm dying to get in—if the class fills up, freshmen are always the first to get cut."

"You're a . . . freshman?" Jessica asked, surprised.

He nodded. "But I might as well start fulfilling requirements since I'm sure about my major."

"Mmmm . . . ," Jessica agreed, envious that Alejandro knew what he wanted.

"I'd love to know about the professors you had last year," Alejandro said earnestly. "I really value the opinion of somebody who knows her way around SVU. There's so much you can't tell from a course catalog, you know?"

Wow, Jessica thought. *He actually wants* my *advice*, my *opinion, on school*. That was a first.

"Well, I definitely owe you big time for helping me get my record straightened out," Jessica told him.

"So maybe I can have your number, just in case I need help planning my schedule?"

"Uh, sure," she said, hoping he wasn't interested in asking her out. She liked Alejandro, but as a friend, not as a date. "Oh—I just realized I don't have a phone yet." *Saved!* "My housemates and I just moved in and—"

Uh-oh.

Housemates.

*   *   *

"So let me get this straight, Mr. Burgess." The Orange County College housing officer folded his hands on the desk and fixed Sam with a stare of barely veiled contempt. "You never sent in your housing application. You never put down a deposit. And you actually think you can waltz into my office a week before classes start and we'll just cough up a room for you?"

Sam slouched down low in his seat, jiggling his knee irritably. He didn't need this pencil pusher acting like his seventh-grade guidance counselor. "Okay, I get it. Everything's full. Could you just take down my name in case you get a cancellation or something?" The housing officer exhaled, making a Darth Vader noise. "I can put you on the waiting list, but I doubt anything will open up before spring. There are plenty of students already wait listed who applied for housing *before* the deadline." He lowered his glasses and looked down his nose at Sam. "Which, may I remind you, was two months ago."

"I know," Sam growled, running a hand through his light brown hair. How could he have missed all the forms he got in the mail? He might be lazy, but he wasn't a moron.

The officer stared uncomprehendingly. "Well, then, Mr. Burgess, that really begs the question of *why* you didn't apply sooner. Don't you have any interest in your own future?"

"Thanks for your time," Sam said. He got up and left the office without another word, slamming the door behind him. He had zero interest in sitting through the lecture he knew by heart, the one his parents and teachers had been giving him for years. So what if he didn't feel like being Mr. On The Ball all the time? Was the world really going to be worse off if he didn't live up to his potential?

Sam trudged back to his battered Ford with his head down and his hands in his pockets. Now he was stuck all on his own to find a place to live. Well, whatever. He didn't expect anybody to cut him any slack. He certainly wasn't about to jump through hoops to get the administration to take pity on him.

Every now and then, now being a perfect example, Sam wondered why he was so hell-bent on not touching the family bankroll that sat in the bank under his name. Instead of getting grief from some pencil pusher, he could be buying a penthouse apartment a block from campus.

If he wanted to, which he didn't.

He used the bare minimum of that money to pay for his very cheap education at OCC and the typical college student's housing and bills. Everyone who met Sam assumed he was totally broke and somehow managed, considering that he didn't have a job. And that was the way he wanted it. *That* was the way he really lived.

In spite of the warm sun beating down on his T-shirted shoulders, Sam felt like his own personal dark cloud was hanging over his head. Stress was one of his least favorite experiences, mostly because he just didn't see the point of it. He had no big drive to achieve great things, at least not right now, and he didn't care what anyone else thought of him. He was living the way he wanted to.

But why did everybody feel the need to point out all the ways he was screwing up his life? If Sam wanted to put the bare minimum of effort into everything he did and deal with the consequences, that was his own business.

"So then I had to go to the bursar's," Jessica was saying as she speared a steamed-pork dumpling between her chopsticks. "And by this time I'm, like, *freaking out*. So I waited in *another* huge line there—and would you believe, they sent me to financial aid?"

Jessica dipped her dumpling in duck sauce and popped it into her mouth, waiting for sympathetic noises. Elizabeth and Neil, sitting on the couch, bent over their takeout cartons, were quiet.

"So get this," Jessica went on when she'd swallowed. "By the time I got to the financial-aid office, they were *closed!* Can you believe it? And after all that, I still have to go back tomorrow to register!"

Glowering, Neil stabbed at a dumpling. Elizabeth swirled her chopsticks around in her carton of noodles, her mouth set in a tight line.

95

Maybe both of them had had a really bad day too.

"I'm leaning toward declaring art history," Jessica went on. "I had the most amazing conversation with this guy I met, the one who helped me at the financial-aid office? But of course I'm still totally stressing about what a huge thing this is to decide all in one day. Can you guys believe I haven't already gone postal?" She frowned. Neil and Elizabeth looked to be verging on postal themselves, the way they were scowling at their food.

Jessica cupped her hands around her mouth like a megaphone. "Hel-*lo!* I'm talking here! Is anybody going to take the slightest interest in my life decisions? Or give me a *tiny* bit of support for the hellish day I had?"

Elizabeth lifted her gaze to meet Jessica's. Her eyes were incredulous and furious at once. "You have *some nerve* complaining about *your* day," she seethed. "Do you know what *we* were doing all day, Jess?"

Instantly on the defensive, Jessica folded her arms across her chest. "Yes, I *do* know—I remembered just before I raced back over here. But don't you think I have a really good excuse for forgetting all day? I mean, come on!"

Her twin's face was turning purple. "You could have called to let us know, Jess. We were interviewing *housemates*—something you should have been interested enough in to remember. And something you promised to be here for. How could you forget something so important? Don't you realize that having our own place is a huge responsibility?"

"Well, excuse me, *Mom*," Jessica snapped, feeling her face heat. Guilt was squirming around inside her, but Jessica squelched it under her annoyance. Okay, maybe she *had* screwed up, but Elizabeth didn't have to lecture her like she was a child. "Did it ever occur to you that I *was* taking care of my responsibilities? I was *enrolling* so I could register, not getting a suntan at the beach or something!"

Elizabeth rolled her eyes, infuriating Jessica. "And did it ever occur to you that we *all* have to register? But somehow *we* magically managed to be home when we said we would. Sometimes I wonder if you *ever* think about anybody but yourself!"

Neil put his hands to his head. "Would you two please calm—"

"I *am* calm!" Jessica shouted at the top of her lungs. "Liz is the one who's getting all—"

"Don't you *dare* put this on me," Elizabeth barked, jabbing a warning finger at Jessica. "Neil is just as mad at you as I am. Right, Neil?"

"I don't want to get—," Neil began.

"Don't put him in the middle of this," Jessica yelled. She was so angry at her sister, she couldn't see straight. It was just like Elizabeth to decide that she had the moral authority to get everyone else on her side. "You're not going to get Neil to gang up on me. He hasn't said anything about being mad!"

Neil groaned. "That's because I can't get a word—"

"Just grow up, Jess, okay?" Elizabeth shook her head. "Just do yourself and everybody else a favor and start acting like an adult."

"I . . . ," Jessica began. Then she saw that Neil had rocketed off the couch.

"That's it! Enough! I can't take any more!" He stalked up the stairs, muttering the whole way. "Twins . . . like living on a damn seesaw . . . What was I thinking?"

"Liz!" Nina blinked in surprise. "Long time, no see."

"Hey, Nina!" Elizabeth exclaimed, holding out her arms for a hug. Her best friend remained standing motionless in the open doorway of her suite. After a second Elizabeth dropped her arms to her sides. "Um, did I catch you at a bad time? I just stopped by to say hi."

"No, no, come on in." Nina held open the door, and Elizabeth stepped into the common room. "Can I get you anything? All I have is water, milk, and soda."

"Thanks, I'm fine. I just needed to get out of the house for a bit. Jess and I got into a fight about house stuff over dinner."

Elizabeth stood hovering in the middle of the room, taking in her surroundings. Nina and her roommate had managed to make the common room feel like a real home. Framed photos covered almost every surface, daisies overflowed from a coffee can on the table, and colorful hanging tapestries obscured the sterile gray cinder-block walls.

Nina, on the other hand, was maintaining a stony silence. "I really like what you've done with this place," Elizabeth offered to fill the air, realizing that it was the kind of thing she would say to her parents' friends. "It's kind of weird to be back at Dickenson now that I don't live here. I almost headed back to my old room out of habit."

"I guess dorm life must seem pretty lame to you now that you have your own place off campus," Nina said.

"What are you talking about?" Elizabeth almost felt like crying. That was way beyond pre-catching-up awkwardness. "Nina, what's going on? Are you mad at me or something?"

Nina pursed her lips and shook her head. "No. No, I'm not mad at you, Liz."

"I know we didn't really keep in touch over the summer," Elizabeth persisted, "but you know I was traveling most of that time. I mean, I barely talked to my own parents. Seriously, Nina, is that it? You know you can tell me anything."

Nina's face contorted into a series of expressions that reminded Elizabeth of someone either lifting weights·or smelling something that had gone bad. Then Nina turned away from Elizabeth and busied herself with rearranging some photographs on a shelf. "It's not you, Liz, really. It's . . . nothing. I'm just . . . tired. From moving in."

Elizabeth chewed the inside of her lip. She wasn't sure whether to feel hurt or worried or both.

Her eyes lit on the pictures Nina was arbitrarily moving an inch to the left. There were a couple of Nina with her parents and several of a girl and guy Elizabeth didn't recognize. Nina's roommate and her boyfriend, she assumed. She glanced around the room and spotted more pictures of the couple, plus several of the guy alone.

Something occurred to Elizabeth.

"Nina," she said, "how are things with Bryan? Are you guys dealing with the transfer thing okay?"

Even from the back, the way Nina stiffened was obvious. "He's fine." The words came out in a staccato monotone. "We're fine."

"Are you sure?" Elizabeth persisted. "I don't mean to pry, but I don't see any pictures of him. You had tons up in your room last year."

Nina was silent, frozen.

"Nina. Look at me."

Slowly Nina turned to face Elizabeth. "We're fine," she repeated. "I just haven't finished unpacking my pictures yet. I still have a lot to do."

Elizabeth felt a pang of sorrow. Why would Nina shut her out like this? Her best friend was acting like a stranger.

"Well, I'll let you get back to work, I guess," Elizabeth said. "It was good to see you, Nina. And if you ever need to talk . . ."

She trailed off. If she actually had to remind Nina that Elizabeth was there for her, then she was probably wasting her breath.

Dana was having a hard time fitting her key in the door to her house with Todd kissing the back of her neck. She finally unlocked the door, and Todd grabbed her by the waist and tossed her over his shoulder.

"Todd!" she protested. "My stomach isn't appreciating this—I ate way too much at dinner!"

They tumbled through the doorway together in a tangle of limbs. Dana was shrieking and laughing as Todd strode down the hallway. "Todd, put me down!"

Suddenly Todd stopped and slid Dana down to her feet. She whirled and saw Molly, Kimiko, and Joyce sitting in the living room. There was something ominous about the way they were arrayed, all three chairs facing in the same direction as if they were sitting in judgment. The room was silent. All eyes were on Dana and Todd.

Molly cleared her throat. "We need to talk."

"Do you guys have a few minutes for a house meeting?" Kimiko asked.

Dana exchanged uneasy looks with Todd. She briefly considered making a break for the bedroom. "Um, sure."

"Todd's been staying here for a couple of weeks now," Joyce began.

"Rent-free," Molly added.

"He ties up the phone, and he doesn't even chip in for the bill," Kimiko said, tossing her red hair.

"*He* is standing right here, and *he* makes all his long-distance calls on his calling card," Todd said with undisguised irritation.

Dana reached for Todd's hand and squeezed it, praying that he would keep his temper in check. Things had been tense enough lately. She didn't need any more friction with her roommates. "Well, I'm sure we can lay down some ground rules for however long Todd's here," she said. "And besides, he's practically already found a place. Right, honey?" She turned to Todd, silently appealing to him to help smooth things over.

He hesitated for too long, and when he spoke, his voice was a little higher than normal. "Um, yeah!" Todd darted a nervous glance at Dana. "I'm really . . . trying hard to find a place."

"Gee, how did you find time to work that in

between going to the gym and watching baseball on TV?" Kimiko asked.

"Not to mention your culinary experiments." Joyce sniffed.

Todd's reddened face was twitching, veins straining to burst from his temples. Dana willed him with all her heart to keep calm.

"And leaving your foul, nasty socks and stuff all over *everything*," Molly added. "At this point I wouldn't be surprised to find jockstraps hanging off the shower rod."

Dana could pinpoint the precise second when Todd snapped. He let go of her hand and snarled at Molly, "Well, it's no picnic for *me* trying to hack my way through that jungle of stretched-out bras and skanky, disgusting underwear you call a bathroom!"

Dana cringed, slapping her palm to her forehead. "I'm sure he didn't mean that," she said through her fingers, knowing nobody was listening.

"Well, *we* live here," Molly pointed out. "So if we want to bake a cake in the bathtub, that's our right. *You*, on the other hand, are totally dependent on our generosity."

Todd sputtered, "Don't give me that—"

"I say we take a vote right now," Joyce said. "All in favor of Todd getting the heck out of here?" She raised her hand in the air.

Molly and Kimiko raised their hands too, glaring at Todd.

Dana gasped. How could her friends put her in this position? "Wait, you guys can't do this! I live here too, you know!"

"Sorry, Dana, but you're outvoted," Kimiko said.

"But . . . but you guys are my friends!" Dana felt tears pricking her eyes. "Don't you realize what a terrible position it puts me in if you throw my boyfriend out on the street?"

"Well, if *you* were a friend, you would have thought of how it made *us* feel to put up with him for two weeks," Joyce countered.

Todd moved closer to Dana. His face was contrite now and a little bit terrified. "Listen, I never meant for it to come to this," he said. "Please, if you could just give me a few days to—"

"Too little, too late," Kimiko cut him off.

Fury welled up inside Dana. "How can you guys be so callous?" she snapped. "I'm not going to let you do this to me! If Todd goes, then I go too!"

As soon as the words were out, they hung in the air like a sword over Dana's head. Molly raised her eyebrows questioningly at Joyce, who nodded. Both of them turned to Kimiko. Kimiko hesitated, then shrugged.

"Fine with us," Molly said at last, clapping. "So it's settled. We'll find another roommate."

Dana's jaw dropped.

*   *   *

"I wouldn't be caught dead wearing a baby bonnet and sucking on a pacifier," Moira said in her usual bored-to-tears voice, reaching for the bowl of popcorn on the coffee table in the Oakley Hall lounge. "I heard that's what Theta made their pledges do last year. And that's exactly why I didn't pledge when I was a freshman—there's no way I'm doing cheesy stunts to join a sorority."

"Lighten up, Moira," Lisa Lewisi retorted, grabbing a handful of cheese puffs. "All the dumb stuff that happens during rush is a tradition. Anyway, what's a few days compared to your whole college career? For four years in the only sorority on campus that matters, I'd wear diapers for a week." The girls clustered in the lounge nodded.

Sitting cross-legged on the floor, Chloe sipped her can of diet soda and glanced back and forth between her floor mates. She wished she could be as confident as Lisa, standing up to Moira like that. Chloe could barely scrape up the nerve to squeak hello to her roommate. The girl had more intimidation tactics than a police-interrogation team.

"I don't think Theta is *the* sorority," Eva put in as she was braiding Anoushka's hair on the lounge couch. "Not everybody is obsessed with wearing the right clothes and being seen with the right people. I pledged Alpha Chi because it seemed like a real community—not a bunch of judgmental snobs."

Alpha Chi was the "alternative" sorority, Chloe recalled. She was intrigued by the sound of it, but she wasn't sure whether she wanted to pledge a sorority at all. Belonging to a group might be reassuring, but it might just put more pressure on her to be someone she wasn't—or didn't want to be. And besides, it would give her mother a little too much satisfaction.

"Theta isn't all about clothes and status," Anoushka said. "My friend Denise is a Theta, and she's a total nonconformist—not hung up on her image at all. She's probably going to be the new president when the government elections are held in a few weeks. Theta's definitely going to be different this year."

"Good—maybe that means they'll have acceptable pledge requirements," Moira cut in. "I might think about pledging after all." The talk then turned to pledging—everyone seemed excited and nervous that rush week was coming up in a few weeks.

And everyone, even the other freshmen, seemed to know everything there was to know about SVU. Chloe felt totally clueless by comparison. She'd been hanging out in the lounge for an hour, but so far she hadn't found a single opening into the conversation.

Moira had the eerie power to look poised even when she was tossing kernels of popcorn into her mouth. "What I hate about sororities like Theta

106

are the fake girls who put on a big phony act like they're so down-to-earth and into the environment. Meanwhile they're totally rich and wear couture T-shirts."

Chloe looked away. Was that remark directed at her?

"Denise isn't stuck-up!" Anoushka protested, turning her head to look at Moira. "And neither are most of her Theta friends!"

"Hold still, Noush—your braid's coming loose," Eva commanded. "Hey, I know some cool Thetas too. I'm just saying I can't get into the whole status trip that most sorority girls are into."

Now that was something Chloe had a strong opinion on. Still, it surprised her a little to hear her own voice pipe up. "I totally agree, Eva."

"Oh, yeah?" Eva was actually looking in her direction. So, it seemed, was everybody else in the room.

Chloe took a deep breath. "Um, yeah," she went on. "I mean, who cares if somebody has money, or wears expensive clothes, or whatever? Just because you—you don't vacation in Aspen, or live on beluga, or . . . whatever, doesn't make you a lesser person."

The room was silent for a beat. "Beluga?" Lisa asked.

Chloe felt her forehead breaking out into beads of sweat. "You—You know, like the caviar?" Her voice was pitched three octaves higher than normal.

Moira made a discreet snorting noise. "Aspen? Beluga? Looks like someone's a shoo-in for Theta. Just be sure to drop all those expensive names while you're pretending you don't care about them." A few of the girls tittered. Chloe was mortified.

"I didn't mean—I wasn't—," she stammered. "I mean, I don't think I'm really the sorority type. Really."

Moira looked like she was about to say something else, but Lisa spoke first, to Chloe's infinite gratitude. "Well, none of this has convinced me in the slightest that Theta's anything but the best. I don't know what planet you guys come from, but I think being elite and exclusive is a *good* thing. And anyone who says differently is just bitter because they're *excluded*."

Everyone in the room started talking at once, bickering back and forth . . . except for Chloe, who had all but resolved never to open her mouth again. Every attempt she made seemed to go wrong. Maybe she really couldn't escape where she came from.

Everyone was still too busy debating the pledge issue to notice when Chloe got to her feet and slipped out of the lounge. As she trudged alone back to her room, she wondered what Theta was actually like. *Now,* not when her mother was in the sorority. But all this talk about money, clothes, status—it sounded exactly like the superficial world she was desperate to outgrow. The world her mother came from. The irony was that *that* world was probably the only one where Chloe even stood a chance of fitting in.

"Dana, can I get you anything at all? A soda? Some chips?" Todd patted the quivering lump of blankets that was curled up at the edge of the motel room's bed. Although Dana couldn't see his face, he gave her a lopsided grin. Maybe he could make her laugh, shake her out of her funk. "Wanna try the vibrating bed? I think I have some quarters in my wallet."

"No." Dana's muffled voice emerged from somewhere under the hideous plaid comforter. "Just leave me alone. You've done enough."

Todd sighed. "Okay. I'm sorry." He got up from the bed and paced the tiny square of stained, threadbare shag carpet, feeling like the world's most pathetic excuse for a man. Dana had been crying in the fetal position for hours, and nothing Todd said or did could make her stop. Every sob or sniffle from the bed was like a knife through his heart.

Todd suppressed the frustrated urge to bang his head against the greasy-looking stucco wall or punch one of the hideous paintings of sad-eyed children in clown suits. Dana had taken him in when he had nowhere else to go, and how had he repaid her? It wasn't bad enough that he'd acted like a deadbeat, that he'd barely bothered to get off his butt and look for his own place. No, he had to push his luck even further and get his girlfriend kicked out of her own home. How could he ever look Dana in the eye after dragging her down to his level of loserdom?

Todd paused at the window and gazed outside. The E-Z-Rest Motel's flashing neon sign flooded the parking lot with waves of nauseating green and yellow light. *A screwup like me belongs in a scummy place like this,* Todd thought. He would have given his right arm before he subjected Dana to such a filthy hole-in-the-wall. She deserved so much better. And if she hadn't been noble enough to stand up for Todd, she would still be living in a nice house instead of crashing at some dive off the highway that charged by the hour.

From the bed Dana let out a long, shuddering breath. Todd felt absolutely awful. He ran over to the bed and dropped to his knees beside Dana's trembling form. "Honey, please. I can't stand to see you like this! Isn't there anything I can do? I feel like the world's biggest jerk!"

Dana poked her head out from under the covers. Her face was red and puffy; her eyes were almost swollen shut. But to Todd she still looked beautiful. "You're not a jerk," she said with a sniffle. "It was my call to say that I'd leave if you did."

Todd reached out and stroked her tangled hair out of her eyes. "And have I told you how

110

incredibly touched I am that you defended me?"

Dana didn't exactly smile, but her doleful look lifted a little. "Only a couple of thousand times."

Todd chuckled. "Move over, sweetie." He lifted himself up, kicked off his shoes, and crawled into bed behind Dana. "Nobody's ever stuck up for me like that," he whispered, snuggling up against her in spoon formation. "It means so much to me that you feel that kind of loyalty to me." He planted a soft kiss in her hair. "Whatever happens, we're in this together. We'll get through this, I promise."

"How?" Dana moaned. "It's way too late to find anything on campus. And I can't afford my own place. My parents aren't exactly made of money either. Where am I going to go?" A fresh wave of sobs shook her body. Todd held her tightly, feeling more helpless than he'd ever felt in his life.

"Dana, I love you so much," he murmured. "Please, don't cry. I swear, everything's going to work out. We'll be fine. I'll figure out something."

"Like what?" Dana wailed. "You couldn't even find a place for yourself!"

Todd winced. *I deserved that*, he told himself.

"I don't know," he admitted. "But I know I'd do anything to make you happy—*anything*. No matter what it takes, Dana, I swear I'll make this up to you."

111

Chapter
Seven

Elizabeth stood outside the registrar's office and thumbtacked a Room for Rent flyer to the bulletin board, then headed back outside for the next heavily traveled stop. In the warm, golden light of late morning the SVU campus seemed like an idyllic place, lined with neat paths and dotted with tidy green squares of lawn. Now that classes would be starting any day, the campus had lost the eerie feel of a ghost town; the quad teemed with students carrying backpacks, books, and papers. Everything was starting to be the way Elizabeth remembered it.

As she headed across campus, past familiar buildings and familiar faces, Elizabeth felt stress-free for the first time since arriving at the duplex. Her life as a sophomore was finally starting to fall into place. They had a phone, hot unbrown water, and electricity, so not only could they stop living like cave dwellers, but they could actually start getting calls about the spare bedroom.

And most important, she'd gotten registration out of the way. Now it was official—she was a journalism major, just like she'd always planned.

Dreamed, she corrected herself. Her writing wasn't just a plan—it was her passion.

Or was it? Elizabeth suddenly realized that she hadn't felt any particular sense of excitement or fulfillment from checking the box that held the key to her life's work. All she felt was relief that she'd crossed one more thing off her list. In spite of promising herself that she'd loosen up and take more chances this year, she'd automatically gone ahead with exactly what was expected of her. She hadn't even hesitated, hadn't even considered any other options.

Well, of course, she assured herself—journalism was what she'd wanted to do all her life.

But what if that very fact was keeping her closed off from other possibilities? What if she would be better off with creative writing . . . or something totally different, for that matter?

Elizabeth reached the student center and scanned the cork bulletin board for stray thumb-tacks. She was beginning to feel a nagging sense of self-doubt. Maybe she wasn't as driven and motivated as everyone thought—maybe she was just programmed to keep moving on a track she'd been following her whole life. She certainly wasn't spontaneous like her sister. Not for the first time, Elizabeth envied Jessica's willingness to follow her impulses. Even though things didn't always work out like her sister expected, at least Jessica had her eyes open to the whole world.

Elizabeth pried several tacks off the corkboard and pushed one through a flyer. She was getting worked up over nothing, she decided. It was only natural that choosing a major would give her a few jitters. But it wasn't like she'd just signed a lifetime contract. She could still take classes in whatever she wanted—expand her horizons. Maybe she'd pick up an arts course catalog and find out about sculpture or photography or something she'd never tried.

Elizabeth was tacking up one last flyer in the student center when a shadow loomed over the bulletin board. "Liz? Is that you?" The deep male voice made the nape of her neck prickle.

No. It couldn't be. What were the odds? But she knew that voice. . . .

She whirled around. It *was* him. He was wearing his infuriatingly cocky crooked grin, his hazel eyes twinkling at her. Memories rushed at her. The arguments, the constant friction . . . and the passionate kisses, the only way Elizabeth had ever found to wipe that smirk off his face.

Tom shifted in the chair that faced his adviser's desk. Usually these little preregistration sessions were drive bys, but he'd been squirming in his seat for a good ten minutes—and the situation looked grim. The creases in Professor Rosenbaum's forehead were gradually deepening as he scanned Tom's registration form. Tom was starting to have second thoughts about his last-ditch effort to get a life.

The professor lifted his eyes to Tom. "I must say I'm a little confused. You don't have a single course here that fulfills any of your journalism requirements."

"I know." Tom sank lower in his chair.

"So how do you plan to make up all those credits?"

Tom stared at his hands. "To tell you the truth, I was thinking about changing majors. If I switch over to English, I'll only need ten credits to complete the major. So I could still take a couple of light semesters and graduate this May."

"But Tom, why would you give up on your goals?" His adviser's face registered horror. "You've already completed so much of your journalism course work! Why set your sights low?"

Tom shrugged. "I've worked really hard my whole college career, and now I want to relax a little. You know, not push myself as much."

"Is it the TV station? Is that taking up too much of your time? Because I'm sure we can find a way to cut down on your hours there. Your education should come first."

"Actually," Tom said, "I was thinking of taking a break from the station."

Professor Rosenbaum turned sheet white. "Tom, I must tell you I am not at all convinced that you're making the right decision. You're proposing to all but abandon everything you've achieved at SVU. What exactly do you plan to *do* with yourself this semester?"

Tom took a deep breath. Maybe he *was* making a huge mistake. It did sound lame that he was ready to ditch everything he'd ever cared about. But what was the point of sticking with it if he didn't care about it anymore?

"Well, I was thinking about rejoining the football team," he admitted. "I've really missed sports, and I'd like to experience being part of a team one more time before I graduate."

Tom braced himself for more of his adviser's alarmed attempts to dissuade him.

But the man was beaming. Actually beaming. "The team—that puts everything in perspective! Why didn't you *say* so? Tom, that's wonderful news. The team hasn't been the same since you left."

"Um, thanks," Tom said tentatively, mildly bewildered by the show of enthusiasm. He'd hoped Professor Rosenbaum would warm to the idea, but he hadn't expected him to do a total 180.

"Of *course* you don't want to overburden

yourself with other activities if you're on the team," the professor went on. "Being quarterback is a hundred-and-ten-percent commitment. Oh, Tom, I'm so pleased—this is a great thing you're doing for SVU. The coach is going to be thrilled. Having you back will raise the whole school's profile."

"You really think so?" Tom sat up straighter in his seat. That wasn't the kind of thing someone would say just to be encouraging.

"Of course! You're a hero on this campus, Tom." Professor Rosenbaum picked up his pen, signed Tom's registration form with a flourish, and handed it back to him. "And listen, if your course load gets to be too much for you to handle on top of your practice schedule, you just let me know. I'm sure we can work something out."

Tom thought of asking what happened to his education coming first. But he wasn't interested in being the devil's-advocate investigative-reporter type anymore. He was all about being a jock now.

"Thanks a lot," Tom said with a grin, getting to his feet. "I'll definitely keep that in mind." He grasped his adviser's outstretched hand and pumped it vigorously, more convinced than ever that he was making the right decision.

It was almost too perfect. Being an athlete was like a free ticket to taking the easy way out. From now on he'd be coasting through the rest of college. Five minutes ago Tom was a slacker, and now he was a hero. Why hadn't he thought of this sooner?

"So then we pull up in the parking lot at Oakley," Eva said, "and he leans across the seat . . . and I swear, you guys, he had a giant chunk of spinach stuck between his teeth! I was so grossed out that I couldn't stop him before he plastered his greasy lips to my mouth and shoved his spinachy tongue practically down my throat!"

Anoushka and Lisa, sitting cross-legged on the floor by Moira's bed beside the empty pizza box, cracked up. Chloe, sitting on her bed with her legs stretched out, laughed too, wishing she had Eva's funny, dramatic way of telling stories. Half of the talent was in Eva's voice, the other half in her expressions.

Moira, of course, found nothing funny about spinach in a guy's teeth. She sat with her knees up and her back against the headboard, shaking her head. "So he takes you to some cheesy steak house—like *anyone* eats red meat anymore—then makes you pay your share of dinner, and then he actually expects you to make out with him, with a glob of green in his teeth, no less? Unbelievable."

"I didn't mind paying my share," Eva said, getting a raised eyebrow from Moira. "Especially because I wasn't interested in going out with him again. But to have him shove his gross tongue in my mouth when all I wanted was to give him a polite good-night, good-bye-forever peck, *that* I minded."

"Yeah," Chloe agreed. She'd been desperate for a witty, entertaining way to join the conversation for the past half hour and *yeah* was the best she could do?

"I don't even kiss on the first date when I *do* like a guy," Lisa said. "Except on the cheek."

"Did you just beam here from 1950?" Moira snorted. "You're kidding, right?"

Lisa dipped a french fry in ketchup and waved it menacingly over her head as if she were about to throw it at Moira.

"I think you have a point, Lise," Eva agreed. "It's better not to show them right away how much you like them. Guys like a challenge."

"You guys have been reading too much *Cosmo*," Anoushka said. "It's not about playing games with the guy—it's about doing what feels right. I went a lot farther than just kissing with my boyfriend on the first date, and we've been together a long time now."

Chloe tried again. "I had the most amazing kiss of my life on a blind date." It was actually true. Last spring when she'd visited SVU, her old family friend Lila Fowler had fixed her up with a supercute guy. They'd gone to dinner and spent hours talking, and Chloe had been filled with an intoxicating sense of possibility . . . a dizzying taste of the independence of college life. Impulsively she'd kissed him good night—an intense, *adult* kiss that actually took her breath away, just the way they said an amazing kiss should.

If she had to be honest with herself, that kiss— and everything it symbolized—was a big reason why she'd ended up at SVU.

"Well, I'm glad it worked for you, Noush," Eva went on obliviously. "My boyfriend had to spring for three dinners before I let him touch me."

"I didn't make Jeff wait *that* long," Lisa said. "I mean, come on—there's a fine line between being a challenge and being a nun. Especially since I didn't want him to forget me once I went off to school."

Did *everyone* have a boyfriend but Chloe? They were all talking like they knew everything there was to know about relationships. Chloe had dated around, but she'd never been involved in anything serious. Actually, the only guy she'd ever felt sparks of real potential with—who'd talked to her about art and books and music instead of sports and Sega Genesis—was the blind-date guy.

"Well, I don't think a relationship is about *letting* the guy do stuff," Anoushka pointed out. "I mean, it should be about what you want. He should be respectful of your needs." Her mouth curled into a devilish smile. "And believe me, my

121

man takes care of my needs." They all burst into laughter.

"My boyfriend is really sensitive too," Chloe said suddenly.

All heads turned toward her. "*You* have a boyfriend?" Moira asked. "How come you never mentioned him before?"

Chloe's heart was hammering. What had possessed her to blurt out that lie? She did her best to shrug. "Um, I don't know—it never came up."

"What's his name?" Anoushka asked, sounding genuinely interested.

"Um. Uh," Chloe stalled, racking her brain. The first name that came to mind was the blind-date guy. "Tom Watts," she supplied.

"*Tom Watts?*" Eva repeated, her voice dripping with disbelief. "As in, former star quarterback, campus news anchor, straight-A student Tom Watts?"

"Uh, yeah," Chloe squeaked, her mind still reeling. She darted a glance at Moira, whose eyebrows were practically grazing her hairline.

Everyone was staring at her, obviously waiting for her to elaborate. Well, at least they weren't ignoring her. But she'd really dug herself into a hole. She had no choice but to keep digging.

Chloe cleared her throat. "We, um . . . a mutual friend fixed us up last spring when I visited SVU. We kept in touch all summer, and then, uh . . . I came here so . . . so we could be closer together."

"Oh, that's so romantic!" Eva exclaimed.

"Ooooh, an upperclassman," Lisa whispered. "I'm impressed. Hey, do you want some fries?" She held out the carton to Chloe.

"Thanks." Chloe extracted a fry, her peripheral vision attuned to Moira. To her astonishment, her roommate was regarding her with something resembling respect. Chloe felt like she'd stumbled on the combination to a safe. Was that all it took—having a boyfriend?

"You're so lucky." Lisa sighed. "Being on the same campus is, like, a huge luxury. When I got into SVU and Jeff got accepted to Boston College, I cried for three days."

"Totally," Anoushka agreed. "Raj goes to USC, and we see each other on weekends, but it's just not the same."

"Yeah, it's so much easier now that we're together," Chloe said. "You know, all summer I had to wonder what Tom was doing, who he was seeing. . . . I mean, not that I don't *totally* trust him since he tells me all the time I'm the only girl for him. But hey, I'm the jealous type."

"Me too," Eva said. "My boyfriend lives right across campus, and I call him all the time to check up on him."

"You know, the great thing about Tom," Chloe said, beginning to feel more at ease, "is if he's going out, he calls *me* to check in."

Eva and Lisa cooed. "That is *so* sweet." Anoushka sighed.

"Isn't it? I couldn't find a sweeter or hotter guy in my wildest dreams." Chloe sat back on her bed and munched her fry. The others looked so convinced, she was starting to believe her own story. So what if she was lying through her teeth? Being herself made her a lot more nervous.

"*What* are you doing here?" Elizabeth asked Sam, stunned by the sight of him.

"Nice to see you too," Sam replied.

"Oh, I mean—I just—" Elizabeth was still blinking, trying to process the way he'd appeared without warning. "I just wasn't expecting to run into you here."

"I had some things to do on your campus. So, how are you doing?" Sam's gaze lingered too long for comfort, and Elizabeth found herself fidgeting. "You look great, Wakefield," he added in a low voice.

"Thanks." Elizabeth felt her face heat. He was as gorgeous as ever, she had to admit to herself— even if she would sooner die than say it aloud. His tan was a slightly lighter shade of golden brown than the last time she'd seen him, and his perpetually unkempt sandy brown hair was sticking up adorably in the back. It irritated her to realize how attractive she found him. There was something suspicious about a guy who could make bed head look charming.

"So, what are you up to?" Again Sam filled the silence, as if it had been days instead of weeks since they'd spoken. "Wanna grab a cup of coffee, catch up a little?"

You have some nerve, Elizabeth seethed silently. All summer long they'd danced around hooking up, unable to stay away from each other in spite of their differences. Sure, they'd agreed it was best to end it—but that didn't mean Sam had to blow her off completely. It was bad enough that he hadn't returned her letter or her phone calls, but now he was acting like nothing had ever happened between them.

"I'm actually kind of busy." Elizabeth shifted the stack of flyers in her arms. "I have to, um, put these up."

"Can I see?" Sam plucked a sheet before Elizabeth could react. "Room for rent, huh? You're looking for a housemate?"

"Well, uh, yeah," Elizabeth said. What did he want from her? If he was so interested in her life, why hadn't he gotten in touch with her? "Jess and Neil and I."

"That's funny," Sam said, meeting her eyes, "because I'm actually looking for a place. I got wait listed for housing at my school. That's why I stopped by SVU—to see if anyone was looking to share an apartment."

"Oh—I don't—you mean—," Elizabeth stammered, racking her brain for a way to tell Sam that pigs would fly before she would live under the same roof with him. His face was impossible to read.

Wait, what was she thinking? This was Sam, the most unreliable guy on the face of the earth. There was no point in telling him to keep his distance when she would probably never hear from him again anyway.

Elizabeth smiled her sweetest smile. "What a coincidence. Why don't you hang on to that flyer and get in touch with us if you're interested?"

"That sounds great." Sam folded the flyer and tucked it into the back pocket of his jeans. His hazel eyes flitted back to Elizabeth and held hers. Unexpectedly he reached out and touched her arm briefly. "It's really good to see you, Liz. Listen, are you free for dinner tonight? I know it's last minute, but I'd really like to catch up with you. And I could stop in and check out the room when I take you home."

Elizabeth's smile dropped a little. The casual intimacy of his gesture had caught her totally off guard. What could she say? "Um, sure."

"Great. What time should I pick you up?" he asked.

"Why don't I just meet you wherever we're going," she responded, wanting to keep whatever this was as casual as possible.

He regarded her for a second, then told her where and when. The restaurant was unfamiliar, but she knew from the address that it was nearby. "Fine," she told him. "I'll see you there."

Sam nodded and walked away, Elizabeth gaping after him. She had no idea what to think. After all this time did Sam Burgess really plan to drop back into her life, just like that? He'd seemed so genuinely glad to see her, so earnest.

What was she thinking? Elizabeth clutched her flyers to her chest and headed for the arts building. Sam probably wouldn't even show up tonight.

"Martin, Neil." Professor Assata, a fortyish woman in a brightly colored African print wrap, smiled at him across the desk. "I'm sorry—I have to admit you don't look familiar to me. You're not a freshman, are you?"

"No, a transfer," Neil answered with a tight smile. "From Stanford." That she clearly hadn't gone over his records yet was a good sign. All through August he'd been tormented by paranoid fantasies that Stanford was sending out campuswide bulletins about him.

"Oh, okay. I didn't think so—you don't have that wide-eyed freshman look." Professor Assata laughed.

Neil wanted to join in, but in spite of her warm, nonintimidating manner he couldn't let himself relax. Not with that thick manila folder sitting on the desk between them like a ticking time bomb. Any minute she'd be asking him the questions he hating answering.

"Okay, let's take a look at your transcript." The professor opened the folder and pored over the first page.

Eyes straining for a glimpse at the computer-printed sheet, Neil wiped his damp palms on his jeans. There was no reason to be nervous, he told himself. There was nothing on paper, no record of what had happened. They'd made absolutely sure of that.

Professor Assata nodded. "These grades are excellent." Her brown eyes searched Neil's face. "May I ask why you left Stanford? Not that SVU isn't a great school, but you were on the dean's list at one of the most prestigious universities in the country."

Neil felt his stomach constrict. "Financial reasons," he said quickly, automatically. "My financial aid fell through."

Her face was quizzical. "Was there some significant change in your family's status?"

Like that my father no longer has a son? Neil wanted to ask. "No," he replied instead, staring at the floor. "They just reduced my aid package for sophomore year."

"Oh, that's a shame," Professor Assata said. "I hate to see an intelligent young person sidetracked for economic reasons. But don't worry—I'm sure you have a bright future ahead of you at SVU."

Neil didn't trust himself to respond. The professor's friendly manner just made it harder to keep up his front. No matter how many times he parroted the same excuses, Neil had the gnawing fear that he'd break down.

And in a way, it would almost be a relief. It was exhausting to build the wall of lies ever higher around himself. Not that his financial status was a lie, he granted himself. But he couldn't stand to think about what this kind, sympathetic woman would think of him if she knew the truth.

"Thanks," he choked out. "I appreciate the vote of confidence. But I'm actually . . . kind of in a hurry. Do you think we could get to my courses for this semester?"

Professor Assata blinked, looking slightly taken aback. "Certainly."

Neil squirmed as the professor reviewed his registration form. He felt like an awful person for being so brusque with the nicest, most understanding adviser he could ever ask for. But that was nothing compared to the humiliation of admitting why he *really* left Stanford. If anyone ever found out . . .

But that wasn't going to happen. Neil wouldn't let it. And besides, it was classified info at Stanford. Even someone digging for information on Neil wouldn't learn of it. From now on, he was going to forget what really happened. Maybe if he told himself often enough that he'd left solely for financial reasons, he would actually believe it. Maybe he'd stop feeling so betrayed. And maybe the ache of loneliness, anger, and regret deep within him would just go away.

Yeah, right, Neil thought. And maybe he'd win the lottery too.

Chapter
Eight

"Thanks for *nothing*," Todd muttered as he trudged down the front steps of the campus housing office, his hands shoved in the pockets of his windbreaker. Okay, so maybe it was more than a little late to be looking for a room on campus. Two months late, to be exact. But did that give the housing officer the right to laugh in his face?

Todd scowled at the ground, his dark mood getting darker because students all around him were enjoying the sunny morning. Everyone else could afford to hang out on the quad all day— they all had dorm rooms to go home to. Unlike Todd, pathetic specimen that he was, who had nothing more than a few bars of soap from the Slea-Z-Rest Motel to call his own.

A sorry excuse for a man—that's what he was, Todd concluded as he headed for the bulletin board outside the housing office. It made him cringe to think of all the times he'd joked with Dana about being an NBA star, about supporting her and treating her like a queen. What a load! He not only couldn't support Dana, he'd actually gotten her kicked out of her home through his own pigheadedness and immaturity.

And now Dana didn't even want his help in finding her a new house share. She'd told him he'd have a hard enough time finding his own place, let alone one for her too. She was probably right.

Todd stopped in front of the bulletin board and scanned the ragged, overlapping layers of flyers. Between ads selling used futons and seeking baby-sitters were a few posted for off-campus housing. His eyes lit on one, half buried under papers, that read: Room for Rent—Spacious, Ocean View, Share Kitchen. Todd brightened; that was perfect! He lifted up the other flyers to read the rest of the ad—and gulped. The asking price was about a thousand dollars more than he could afford.

He kept looking, leafing under layers of paper. One place was dirt cheap, but the paper was so yellowed and rain battered that Todd assumed the posting had been there since last fall's semester.

Then he spotted an affordable share in a duplex—great! But as he was about to tear off the phone number, he saw the words, *Ask for Liz, Jess, or Neil.* Todd drew back his hand as if he'd been burned. He had more than enough problems without moving in with his ex-girlfriend—the way-too-judgmental Elizabeth. They'd been a couple all through junior high and high school and had managed to break up about five seconds into their freshman year at SVU.

Plus before he'd met Dana, she'd had a fling with another of Elizabeth's ex-boyfriends, Tom Watts, while Tom and Elizabeth had been broken up. He didn't think Dana would be too into hanging out at his place if Elizabeth Wakefield lived there too.

Todd was ready to start banging his head against the bulletin board in frustration. Everything was out of his price range—even the places that sounded like dives cost twice as much as he could afford to pay. And Dana, he knew, was in the same boat.

Todd clenched his hands into fists, hating how powerless he felt. He would sooner die than break his promise to make things up to Dana. But *how* could he make things up to her? How could he take care of two people when he couldn't even afford half of one person's rent?

Then all at once the numbers in his head started to rearrange, adding up to a possibility he hadn't considered. He stared at the flyers in a new light, dividing the impossibly large rents in half. A one-bedroom split two ways—now this he could manage. Not all of them, sure, but some were definitely doable.

Todd was overcome with a dizzying mix of

elation and apprehension. Could he? Should they? Maybe it would be totally jumping the gun—and premature commitment usually spelled relationship death.

But they'd gotten along so perfectly when he stayed at her apartment. And the thought of coming home to Dana every night made Todd very, very happy.

He started tearing phone numbers from flyers, the wheels of his mind spinning. Maybe he couldn't exactly *provide* for Dana just yet. But at least he could show her how committed he was to her—and give her a taste of their adult life together. If any couple was ready to take the plunge and move in together, it was he and Dana.

"Finally I got Jessica and Neil to agree that their tchotchkes could coexist peacefully." Elizabeth was swirling her spoon in a mug where the cappuccino had long since become one with the whipped cream. "And in a matter of minutes they were arguing over what color curtains would match the daisy lights *and* the hula lamp."

Nina nodded, her tension apparent even in the low light of the coffeehouse. Despite the din of the students at surrounding tables, Elizabeth felt her friend's silence reverberating in her ears.

"Can you believe those two? Isn't that just so typical?" Elizabeth was talking just to talk. It seemed like she'd been babbling for hours, inane details about household hassles that were tedious even when they were happening. But her questions to Nina had yielded only monosyllables, and Elizabeth couldn't stand any more awkward pauses.

Nina smiled unconvincingly. "Typical. Sure."

"And don't even get me started about the paint-color conversation," Elizabeth added, feeling like an idiot.

Any pretense of a smile had left Nina's face. She set down her espresso and fixed Elizabeth with an exasperated look. "Listen, Liz, you don't have to fill me in on *every* exciting detail of your cool off-campus life. If you're trying to make me feel included, don't bother. I know I'm dull compared to all your cool TV-road-trip friends."

"What are you talking about?" Elizabeth practically flung her cappuccino mug onto the table, where it teetered in the saucer, liquid slopping over the side. "Nina, I invited you for coffee because I wanted to catch up—because I missed you. Do you really think I'm the kind of person who would let something like being on TV go to my head?"

Nina put her fingers to her temples and squeezed her eyes shut. "No. You're right. I'm sorry, Liz. It's just that you have this big, fun off-campus house . . . and I'm all alone in the dorms."

"No, you're not—you have a suite mate," Elizabeth pointed out. "Maybe you guys will get to be good friends. Who knows?"

"It's not that. I mean alone like—" Nina stopped herself and waved her hands as if to clear the air. "Listen, never mind. Forget I said anything. Anyway, what were you going to say about the paint?"

"Oh, no, you're not getting off that easy. This is like the most you've opened up to me since we got back to school." Elizabeth leaned forward and touched Nina's hand. "Alone like what? What do you mean, Nina?"

Nina stared into her espresso mug. Elizabeth sensed she was on the verge of crumbling. Whatever pain she was in had been building up inside her for a long time.

"It's Bryan, isn't it?" Elizabeth pushed on. "I saw how you reacted when I brought him up the other day. See, you can't even look at me! Nina, come on—you'll feel so much better if you just let it out!"

"All right!" Nina threw up her hands in surrender. "Turn off the interrogation lamp—I'll spill." She released a weary sigh, her shoulders slumping. "Remember last year, when I kept getting suspicious that Bryan was cheating on me? And he swore up and down that I was just being paranoid?"

Elizabeth nodded, her heart already aching for Nina. It didn't take a rocket scientist to figure out where this was headed.

Another deep sigh. "Well, this summer I caught him with her. And the worst part was, he . . ." Nina's voice faltered. "He . . . he didn't even apologize. Just looked me right in the eye—with her clinging to him—and said it was over." Her face jerked in a loud sniffle. "Liz, he transferred to Riverside to be with her! After all we went through together—how could he do this to me?" She covered her face with her hands, her shoulders shaking with sobs.

Elizabeth got up and slid into the seat next to Nina's. "Oh, Nina, I'm so sorry," she murmured, draping her arm across Nina's back.

"I wish I'd never caught him," Nina wailed. "I'd rather be in denial and happy than alone and miserable."

Elizabeth rubbed Nina's back. "You don't mean that, Nina. You're one of the strongest people I know! Listen, this might be the last thing you want to hear right now, but give it time. I know you'll get through this—talking about it was the first step. Don't you feel a teensy bit better since you let it all out?"

"Maybe a little," Nina whimpered. But her face remained buried in her hands.

"Well, I know *I* do. You know, you were really freaking me out with that silent treatment." Elizabeth felt her own eyes filling up with tears— from sympathy for Nina and relief that her friend was actually speaking to her.

"You know," Elizabeth told Nina, "I'm kind of scared about facing this year without a boyfriend too. Tom and I were inseparable last year, and before that there was always Todd." The tears began to flow. "I don't know what I would've done if . . . if I lost you too!"

Nina lifted her wet face to Elizabeth. "Liz, don't cry! I'm so sorry—I had no right to take out all my hurt feelings on you. Bryan's the one who ditched me, not you." She threw her arms around Elizabeth's neck.

They sat clinging to each other and crying for a few seconds, then drew back and burst out laughing.

"We're such dorks," Nina said, grinning through her tears. "I'm so glad you're still my friend, Liz."

"Don't ever freeze me out like that again," Elizabeth pleaded. "Times like these are when we're supposed to turn to each other."

Nina reached for a napkin and blew her nose. "It's a deal. But only if you promise to stop being right all the time."

"Sorry, I can't help you there," Elizabeth declared. "I *know* I'm right—things will get better. We're both going to be just fine without boyfriends holding us back. I mean, come on . . . two intelligent, independent, not to mention totally hot women like ourselves? We're going to have a blast this year."

"Sure, maybe *you* will," Nina said. "I'll be schlepping back and forth from the library to the dorm, with no human contact except for my suite mate constantly telling me how her boyfriend is God's gift."

Elizabeth hesitated for only a split second. "Nina, I would have to check with Jess and Neil . . . but I'm sure it would be no problem for you to take the fourth bedroom at the duplex. I'd love to have you there, if you're into it."

Nina smiled a reassuringly Nina-like smile. "Thanks, Liz. That means a lot. But I think if I'm this scared to be alone, I'd better deal with that. I have to get used to just being on my own for a while—find out what it's like to be just Nina, not part of Bryan-and-Nina."

"I totally understand." Elizabeth nodded. To herself she added the whole truth—that she understood all too well because it was exactly how she felt about being back on campus boyfriendless. Last year she'd practically been an extension of Tom; now she had to figure out who she was, Elizabeth Wakefield, herself.

She was definitely scared, but *good* scared. And Elizabeth had a feeling that Nina would get to good scared pretty quickly.

Tom was panting hard when he finished his tenth lap across the football field. He staggered over to the bleachers and bent over with his palms propped on his thighs, savoring every heaving breath. His lungs felt so much more spacious, his breathing so much deeper, since he'd started training again. It was as if his body had been half asleep all this time, operating at half capacity. With every day he became a little more whole.

Tom wiped the sweat from his brow and tossed back the slick curls of hair that were hanging down in his face. This was so much more satisfying than going to the gym. Every pore of his body was hungrily absorbing the warm midday sun overhead. The fresh air smelled so clean, he could almost ignore the fact that he himself reeked of sweat.

He dropped to the ground and lowered himself into a push-up. Two, three, four . . . his whole body was one solid line of energy, pumping up and down in time. It was incredible to feel so focused, so one pointed. Last year his mind was always a jumble of stresses: schoolwork, WSVU, Elizabeth. . . . Now there was no thought, just pure drive.

Ten, eleven, twelve . . . Tom's arm muscles were beginning to quiver with the effort, but he kept pushing. He still had a long way to go before he got up to peak performance. The coach had gladly welcomed him back on the team, after only a perfunctory tryout—a special case, he'd called it—but Tom wasn't about to coast on past glories.

If he was really going to be a star quarterback again, he had to earn it. There was so much strength in him that had been dormant for months and months—he just had to tap into it again.

Finally Tom collapsed onto the grass, every muscle in his body giving way. He allowed himself a minute to stretch his muscles before dragging himself up to his feet again. And then he was off like a shot once more.

His exhaustion didn't matter. Nothing mattered. All that existed was adrenaline. It felt so good to purify his mind and body, to throw himself into a challenge like this. Tom felt like a different person.

"And the next day Tom showed up at my doorstep with a big bouquet of roses!" Chloe declared, putting her hands across her heart. She fell back against the lounge couch with a dreamy sigh, picturing the scene so vividly that it almost seemed like an actual memory. She did recall seeing something like it in an old movie once. "He flew all that way to surprise me! Don't I have the sweetest boyfriend in the entire world?"

"That is sooo romantic," Lisa whispered.

Eva, and a couple of freshman girls sitting by her on the floor, nodded. Moira looked away.

A gawky guy in thick-rimmed glasses and a Hawaiian shirt was sitting on the couch next to Anoushka, eating a bag of sour-cream pork rinds. "Please don't tell my girlfriend that story," he said, grinning goofily at Chloe. "Guys like that spoil the curve for the rest of us."

"Shut up, Winston." Anoushka elbowed him in

the ribs. "So what happened, Chloe? How long did he stay for?"

"All we had was that one perfect summer weekend together. We barely left each other's side." Chloe gazed off into the distance, loving every second of how her floor mates hung on each word. "After that the weeks were like torture. You can't believe how happy I was when I finally got to campus and saw him again."

"That's funny." Moira's eyes were fixed unblinkingly on Chloe. "You'd think you two would be together all the time. But I don't remember you being out late once since you got here."

Chloe's mouth went dry. All at once she wished desperately that she *weren't* the center of attention. "Uh, Tom's been . . . um . . ."

"I heard he joined the football team again," Lisa said. "That's so cool!"

Chloe could have kissed her. "I know!" she exclaimed. "So he's been training really hard, getting up early, all that stuff. I mean, of course I'm bummed when he crashes at ten P.M., but I'm really proud of him."

"I might actually start going to football games again," Eva said, flopping back onto the floor of the lounge with her arms pillowed under her head. "Chloe, your boyfriend is like a legend at SVU."

Chloe beamed. She really was the luckiest girl in the world. Not only was her imaginary boyfriend gorgeous and sweet, he was a football star to boot.

The gawky guy on the couch froze with a handful of pork rinds halfway to his mouth. "Wait, is this Tom Watts we're talking about?"

Chloe got a bad feeling from the familiar way he said Tom's name. "Yeah, Tom Watts . . . my boyfriend?"

"What a coincidence! I'm Winston Egbert—I know Tom. We both live in the same dorm, but we don't really hang out much anymore. I never see him at Reid—probably because he's always with you and those football players he hangs out with now. What did you say your name was? Zoe?"

"Chloe." She had a terrible sinking feeling. Like this was not good. Not good at all. "Winston, *riiight*," she added quickly. "I think he's mentioned you."

Chloe was starting to sweat. It would look really suspicious if she bolted—but if she stuck around, Winston was bound to catch her in a lie about Tom.

Then again, Winston did say he didn't hang out with Tom. That meant Winston probably didn't know enough about Tom's life to catch her in a lie. It also meant he probably wouldn't go up to Tom at Reid and gush about how he'd met Tom's nonexistent girlfriend.

Reid! All of a sudden Chloe realized that Winston had mentioned where Tom lived!

Bingo!

"Lila!" Jessica threw her arms around her best friend's neck. "I'm so happy to see you!"

Lila Fowler returned the hug for approximately ten seconds before disengaging. "It's wonderful to see you too, but let's not wrinkle the Prada, okay?" She took a step back and smoothed down her perfect pink cashmere twinset and gray pants.

"It's nice to know you never change, Li," Jessica said, grinning. "But it's very nice to see that Theta house has." From where she stood in the doorway, Jessica could see her sorority sisters hanging out—actually looking like they were enjoying each other's company. Last year the sisters were mostly into ruining other people's lives.

"I can't wait to show you what I've done to Alison's old room," Lila said, pulling Jessica inside and leading her down the hall. "It is so fabulous." Lila disappeared into a doorway, and Jessica followed her to the threshold of a huge bedroom.

"Wow," Jessica whispered, leaning against the door frame as she took in the picture window, the large wrought-iron bed with the gauzy canopy, the gorgeous oriental rug. "This is amazing. Alison always had so much stuff thrown around that you couldn't even tell how nice this room was."

144

She shuddered at the thought of Alison Quinn, last year's Theta vice president, who'd gone out of her way to make Jessica's life miserable. Every problem Jessica faced, Alison made it her business to spread it around, just to make Jessica look bad. When Jessica was kicked out of the sorority during an emotional crisis, the whole experience had left her so bitter, she wasn't sure she wanted to come back. But now it was starting to sink in that Alison and her friends were gone.

Jessica sniffed a bouquet of yellow roses that overflowed from a crystal vase on Lila's nightstand. "Aren't you worried that Alison's bad karma is going to rub off on you now that you have her old room?"

Lila made an "as if" expression. "*I* have dominant karma. Besides, I cleaned this room really thoroughly."

Jessica snorted. "Don't you mean you *hired people* to clean it? The last time I checked, Lila Fowler and menial labor don't mix."

Lila lifted her chin and looked down her nose at Jessica. "For your information, last Saturday we had a big cleaning session. The whole house pitched in, and we threw out all the stuff that the sisters who either transferred or graduated left here. It was a total bonding experience."

"I must say, Lila, I'm impressed. Okay, so where are my buddies? I can't wait to see them!"

"They're all hanging out in the *draawwwing*

room," Lila trilled in her best imitation of Alison's pseudo-British affectation, linking her arm around Jessica's. They burst into cackles as they made their way to the drawing room.

The first thing Jessica noticed was the light streaming through the windows. Alison had always insisted on keeping the blinds down so the furniture wouldn't fade. Now they were drawn, revealing the dandelion-dotted green of the Theta garden outside. Jessica blinked and registered the row of girls, talking, flipping through course catalogs, and just hanging out. When they looked up, she saw two of them were Denise Waters and Alexandra Rollins. "Jess! Hi!" they cried, jumping to their feet.

"How are you, Jess?" Denise folded her into a huge bear hug, then surveyed her at arm's length. "You look great!"

"You too—I love those jeans!" Jessica found herself bubbling over with laughter, even though nobody had said anything funny. She hadn't realized how much she missed her friends.

"Hey, Jess!" Alexandra hugged her in turn. "It's good to have you back."

Jessica grinned. "Hey, it's the artist formerly known as Enid!"

Alex, who'd switched to using her middle name at the beginning of freshman year, rolled her eyes. "Very funny, Jess. On second thought, maybe it's *not* so great having you around."

"Oh, c'mon." Jessica squeezed Alex's shoulder. "If I wasn't here to give you a hard time, who would?"

"I think that was her point, Jessica," Lila said.

The other two girls on the couch, who looked young even for freshmen, were looking with interest at her. "Is this the Jessica you were telling us about?" one of them, a petite blonde, asked.

"Are you really an art-history major?" the other girl, a ponytailed Asian in a black slip dress, chimed in. "That's what I'm thinking of doing— I'd love to ask you a bunch of questions sometime, if that's okay."

"Uh . . . sure." Jessica was befuddled. How did they know so much about her? Oh, right— she'd mentioned her registration saga to Denise over the phone and explained her random last-minute decision to pick art history.

"Jess, this is Jackie and May-Ling," Alex explained. "They're rushing Theta this fall."

"Oh, that's great," Jessica said. "I'm sure you'll have a great time—rush is always a blast."

"I can't wait," Jackie agreed. "It seems like all the coolest girls on campus are Thetas."

"Honestly, there were a couple of people who seemed a little snooty when I visited last year," May-Ling admitted. "But now that all you guys are going to be running things, I'm totally into Theta." She gave Jessica an earnest, eager smile. "So, what are you running for?"

"Running for?" Jessica repeated.

147

"Obviously nothing, if you spaced on elections," Lila asserted, sounding like she was only half kidding. "Which is fine by me—not that *anyone* could beat me out for treasurer, but I don't need the competition."

Alex rolled her eyes. "It's not like there aren't plenty of openings—vice president, treasurer, pledge chair. . . ."

"You should run for pledge chair, Jess!" Denise exclaimed. "You're so good at talking to people and planning parties and events and stuff—it'd be perfect!"

Pledge chair did sound great—less like a full-time, year-round job and more like a social thing.

May-Ling's voice broke her train of thought. "So, Jess, tell me about the art-history department," she urged. "Are there any classes I should definitely make sure to take?"

Jessica was about to say that she had no clue; she'd taken only the basic art-history-101 course last year. But then she saw the way May-Ling and Jackie were gazing at her—with that rapt look Jessica used to give older girls during *her* freshman year. And suddenly she realized that taking on a role like pledge chair would mean the responsibility of dozens of girls seeing her that way.

The prospect seemed a little thrilling—and a little unnerving. It was weird to think of anyone looking up to her. Weird, but nice.

*   *   *

"I wasn't expecting such a fancy restaurant," Elizabeth said, setting down her wineglass. She gestured at the candles and flowers on the table, the chandelier overhead. "This place is so expensive."

"What, you figured my idea of a big night out was supersizing a burger combo?" Sam tried hard not to notice her lips, how moist they looked after her sip of wine. "I wanted to do something nice, Liz. I haven't seen you in a long time."

Elizabeth looked taken aback. "I . . . never mind. Forget I said anything." She looked away, winding a lock of silky blond hair anxiously around her index finger.

Sam watched Elizabeth from over the rim of his wineglass as she studied her menu. He hadn't quite figured out why she was so on edge.

She looked beautiful, in any case. Her pale pink sweater was conservative but hugged her curves quite nicely, and her black jeans fitted snugly enough that he wondered if she had borrowed them from Jessica. It occurred to Sam that the outfit was the kind a girl would wear when she was trying very hard not to look like she was trying too hard.

"What?" Elizabeth asked. "Why are you staring at me like that?"

"I was just thinking you look great tonight," Sam answered. The truth. "It's really good to see you, Elizabeth."

"Oh, really." A challenge in her voice.

"Yeah, really," Sam said, looking her straight in the eyes. "Even though things didn't exactly work out between us, I always considered you a friend. A good friend."

"That's funny." Her face was still soft in the candlelight, but her voice was steely. "The last time I checked, friends don't just disappear. You haven't bothered to get in touch with me, Jess, or Neil once since the trip ended."

Sam suppressed the urge to groan. Why did everything have to be such an uphill battle with Elizabeth? He put in twice as much effort with her as he did with any other girl he knew, and it still wasn't enough. "Look, I just had a lot going on after I got back home. Believe me, it wasn't personal—if we end up living under the same roof, you'll see that I'm consistently bad about getting back to people."

Elizabeth's eyes were narrowed. "Is that what this is about? The apartment?"

"What?"

"All this 'I've missed you' stuff." Elizabeth scowled. "Are you trying to schmooze me to get the room? I mean, come on, Sam—I called you twice after the road trip. I wrote you a letter. I didn't hear from you all that time, and now that I have something you want, you're totally into me."

"You have *got* to be kidding." Sam stared into

Elizabeth's furious face. She was actually serious—she held him responsible for not returning a couple of calls, when they weren't even dating. He shook his head in disbelief. "Well, if you think I'm such a scam artist, why did you agree to see me tonight?"

Elizabeth didn't say anything.

Sam blew out a weary breath and rolled his eyes. "Listen, Liz, that's just the way I am. It doesn't mean that I don't like you or don't want to hang out with you. But if it's going to drive you nuts that I don't always return calls promptly or send postcards when I go away, then you might not want me in your apartment."

Elizabeth's mouth hung open in a shell-shocked expression. Sam resisted the urge to buy into her guilt trip. He didn't have time for all her high-maintenance drama when he was just trying to be a nice guy and maybe find a place to live. Elizabeth was the kind of person who always wanted to dig under the surface, who always wanted to look for deep reasons instead of just letting things be the way they were. Sam couldn't deal with that at all.

"Sam, it's not that I don't want to be friends with you," Elizabeth said, sounding repentant. "It just . . . bothered me when we . . . when none of us heard from you after this summer."

We. Not *I.* Who did she think she was kidding? It was obvious where this was headed—a rehash of their *non*relationship. Sam closed his eyes briefly.

He could feel his guard going up, gliding into place like the window of a car. As if they hadn't spent enough time making a big deal about a few incidents of high-school-level fooling around.

"Listen, Liz, it's been a long week—I don't want to get into a whole thing with you right now." He pushed back his chair, dug into his pockets, and threw some bills on the table. "Why don't you think about whether you can deal with having somebody like me living under the same roof. I'll call you in a few days about the apartment."

Sam turned and strode out of the restaurant without waiting for a response. Let her read whatever she wanted into that. If Elizabeth felt like wasting her time overanalyzing someone like him, that was her problem. He'd never given her any reason to have anything but the lowest expectations of him. And he wasn't going to start now.

"Can I take this thing off now? It's starting to itch," Dana complained, her outstretched arms fumbling in front of her.

"If you're referring to any item of clothing *except* the blindfold, be my guest," Todd replied, steering her by the shoulder. "Otherwise you just have to wait a few more minutes. Oh—watch your step."

Dana, unable to see a thing, narrowly managed to avoid tripping over a curb. Where was he taking her? It wasn't her birthday or anything. She shuffled forward, not exactly enjoying this. Dana liked to be in control, to be aware of everything going on around her. The half hour drive here, wherever *here* was, had been excruciating. If she hadn't trusted Todd with all her heart, she would have torn the bandanna from her face and demanded he turn the car around ten minutes into it.

She felt gravel under her feet, then cement again. "Can I look now?" she asked.

"Give me one sec." From Todd's direction came the jangling of keys, then the creak of a door. "Here—this way. Watch your step; we have to go up some stairs."

"*Stairs?* You didn't say anything about stairs," Dana grumbled.

"It's okay. I've got you." Todd clasped her hand and placed his free hand on her back. Dana walked up the seemingly interminable flight of stairs, awkwardly feeling for the steps with her feet. She heard more key noises, then another creaking door.

"Okay, you can look now." Todd whisked the bandanna off Dana's face. *Huh?* They were standing in a tiny kitchen with yellowed flowering wallpaper and a worn linoleum floor. Greasy-looking wooden cabinets, encrusted with fossilized spatters of food, hung over the ancient stove and scarred countertop.

"I don't get it." Dana wandered through the

open kitchen doorway into a small, bare square of a room with chipping, off-white walls. Two windows looked out onto an alleyway. Two open doors revealed an even smaller square of room, carpeted in a hideous maroon, and a narrow bathroom. "What . . . where are we?" Dana asked.

"We're home," Todd said. He pressed his chest against her back and rested his chin on the crown of her head. "*Our* home."

"Todd, what are you talking about?" Dana whirled to face him. "We never even talked about moving in together! Did you actually put down a deposit on this place without discussing it with me? How could you do that?"

Todd's face fell. Instantly she regretted her outburst.

"I just wanted to surprise you," he said in a small, hurt voice Dana had never heard before. "To take care of everything so you wouldn't have to deal. I thought you'd be as excited about living together as I am. But I'll call the landlady and ask her if it's too late to get the deposit back."

"Oh, Todd!" Dana cried, her heart swelling. She grabbed Todd's arms, pulled him close, and planted a cluster of quick, feverish kisses on his face. "I'm not saying I definitely *don't* want to do it—you just caught me off guard. I mean, moving in together is, like, a giant step. I don't even know where we *are,* and you're telling me we're going to live here!"

"We're on Bedford Street, on the outskirts of town—forty minutes to campus by express bus." Todd's face had relaxed a little. He slipped his arms around her waist. "Listen, maybe the surprise factor was a bad idea. I'm really sorry, Dana. But will you at least think about it? I mean, aside from the financial advantages of living together, I think we'd both be incredibly happy. Didn't we get along great while I was staying at your place, except for your housemates? And this would be just us—all the privacy we wanted."

"That *would* be amazing," Dana murmured. It was beginning to sink in: she and Todd, together all the time, with no distractions. Waking up to Todd, coming home to Todd, falling asleep in Todd's arms every night . . . and *not* in a sleazy motel. It sounded like sheer bliss.

"But what if we're not ready for the pressure?" she asked, turning anxious eyes on Todd. "What if it's too much of a good thing too soon? And there's so much else to think about—the bills, furniture, what our parents will say, living so far from campus. . . ."

Todd squeezed her tight in his arms. "I know it's a major decision. I'm worried about all those things too. But the one thing I'm *not* worried about is us. Dana, I've never felt as sure about anything as I do about our relationship. I love you so much. As long as we're together, we can work out everything else."

155

A million more questions deadlocked on the tip of Dana's tongue. This was so sudden, so scary. But at the same time it seemed so perfect. Todd was right—they belonged together. Dana had never felt anything as strong or as deep as the connection between them.

She'd trusted him enough to follow him here blindly. And if she moved in with him, it would be with her eyes wide open. Living together might be hard—but in another way it would be the easiest, most natural thing in the world. By now she'd grown so accustomed to Todd's presence, his body beside hers, that the idea of sleeping alone made her ache.

The more she considered it, the more it was exactly what she wanted. She and Todd, there for each other, through thick and thin.

"Okay, I think we can do this," Dana said, nodding slowly. "I think this is definitely doable."

Todd's face broke out into a wide, beaming grin, like a little kid's. "Dana, you have just made me the happiest guy on the face of the earth. And you know why?"

Dana was grinning too, hugely. "Why?"

"Because there is no way in hell that the landlady was going to give me back that deposit." Todd winked at her.

"You're evil," Dana told him, right before she pulled his face close and crushed his lips to hers in a kiss that was urgent and tender at the same time. Todd's fingers were in her hair; her hands slipped under his T-shirt and slid up his back.

All Dana's worries melted in a surge of warmth as the kiss sent shivers through her whole body. Why had she even hesitated for a second?

Chapter Nine

"You wouldn't believe how different everything is at Theta," Jessica was saying, not so much *to* Elizabeth but *at* her, as they crossed the quad on the way to the campus bookstore. "Now that Alison Quinn's gone, that whole catty, competitive thing is totally history. It's like a real sisterhood, you know?"

"Yeah," Elizabeth said. Whenever Jessica started babbling about Theta stuff, Elizabeth automatically tuned out—otherwise they ended up having the same stupid argument about whether or not sororities were a sexist, shallow waste of time.

"These freshman girls were hanging out, talking about how psyched they were to pledge," Jessica went on. "And they kept asking me questions and listening really closely to everything I said . . . like I was this big authority."

159

"Uh-huh." Elizabeth was trying to calculate mentally how much she would have to shell out for course books. But other thoughts kept intruding. She couldn't stop stewing over the way Sam had just walked out on her last night at dinner. He said he wanted to be her friend, and then the second she brought up something important, he just took off. Who did he think he was?

"And then a bunch of other Thetas came in, and everyone started telling me I should run for pledge chair, that I would do such a great job." Jessica sighed and shook her head. "I was really moved. They all seemed to believe I could do it."

"That's great, Jess." Elizabeth gazed into space, still picturing the way Sam had looked at her—as if he thought she was childish for daring to call him on his inconsistencies. Well, *he* was the childish one for playing those little games with her emotions, for thinking he could just pop in and out of her life as he pleased.

"But the thing is, I'm not sure I can deal. I mean, pledge chair is a ton of work. And there's a lot of other stuff I want to do this semester." Jessica paused for breath. "What if I get sucked into spending all my time on Theta activities and I miss out on something else I really care about . . . something I haven't even discovered yet?"

If only she hadn't let Sam have the last word, Elizabeth thought. It was maddening to know that she'd never get the chance to tell him exactly what she thought of him. Because he certainly wasn't going to call her back about the apartment now, not after last night.

Or would he?

No, of course not. It was obvious to both of them that living together would be pure torture. And it was better that she never speak to him again anyway. With all she had to do, concentrate on, and think about, why add living with Sam to the heaping pile?

Or the effort of fighting her attraction to him.

Elizabeth felt an elbow jab her in the ribs. She glanced up, startled. "Liz! Are you listening? I said look over there!" Jessica tilted her chin.

"What . . ." Elizabeth followed the direction her sister was indicating. All she saw was some guy in a football uniform. Then her eyes practically popped out of their sockets.

Tom Watts.

Tom had spotted her too. A million emotions hit her as she stared into Tom's familiar face, made alien by the hulking shoulders of his uniform. Rejoining the team—that went against everything Tom always told her about how shallow he'd been in those days. How could he change so much in a few months?

She searched his eyes but saw nothing except indifference in them. His face showed no sign that he felt anything at seeing her again.

161

And then, in an instant, it was over. They had passed without speaking.

Jessica squeezed her shoulder. "You all right?" Elizabeth hesitated before answering, searching inside for the part of her that felt hurt, disappointed, regretful—the part that missed Tom. But it wasn't there.

"Yeah," she said finally. "I'm actually fine."

"Are you sure?" Jessica tugged at Elizabeth's sweater sleeve. "That must have been pretty intense. I mean, I always thought that you and Tom would eventually hook back up. But after seeing that little deep freeze, I guess it's really over for good."

"It is kind of weird to know that I'm not in love with Tom anymore," Elizabeth agreed. "But you know what's even weirder?"

"That Tom Watts, boy reporter, has morphed into Tom Watts, superjock?" Jessica offered.

Elizabeth giggled and hooked her arm around her twin's, suddenly feeling as if a weight had been lifted from her. "That too. But what I was going to say was—I was kind of freaked out about coming back to SVU alone, without a boyfriend for the first time. But it really feels okay."

The whole way back to his dorm, Tom couldn't get that look on Elizabeth's face out of his mind. The exhilaration he'd felt after his first uniformed practice was gone, replaced by a sour feeling.

162

He couldn't help wondering whether it was disgust, shock, or pure apathy that had registered in her expression when she saw him in uniform. But he had to admit to himself he'd probably never know. The Tom Watts that Elizabeth had been drawn to was gone—he'd reverted back to a chapter of his life that she played no part in. And it was easier that way. There was no room for a prissy, neurotic downer like Elizabeth Wakefield in Wildman Watts's world.

Tom scowled at the ground as he strode across campus. He'd have to remember to keep telling himself that. Maybe once the season started—once he saw the fans in the bleachers and the sorority girls at the victory parties—he'd actually believe it.

"Tom?" A red-haired girl was lying on the grassy quad in front of Reid Hall, shielding her eyes with a music magazine. "Tom Watts, right?"

Tom slowed to a stop and stared at the girl. It took him a second to place her—the worn plaid-flannel shirt, thin camisole, and threadbare jeans threw him off. She was almost unrecognizable as the elegant girl in the silk dress who'd gone to finishing school with Lila Fowler. "Uh . . . Cody?" he asked tentatively.

"Close—you almost remembered! It's Chloe," she said, her smile huge. "Wow, I can't believe I actually saw someone I know! This is such a coincidence—what are you up to?"

"I was just heading home—I live here,"

Tom explained, gesturing toward the dorm.

"Oh, this is a dorm! I wasn't really sure—this grassy area just looked like a nice, sunny spot to collapse and do some reading." Chloe laughed, flashing a dimple in her cheek. There was something almost forced about that laugh. She seemed nervous about something. "So, how's your roommate? Do you guys get along?"

"No roommate—I've got a single this year," Tom replied, trying to read her. Did she feel awkward about seeing him? He flashed back to their kiss—a surprisingly passionate good night for a blind date he'd gone on only as a favor to Lila. But then, Chloe had surprised him all night—mature for a high-school student and interesting for a friend of Lila's. Tom remembered thinking he wouldn't mind seeing her again if she ended up at SVU, but she hadn't crossed his mind since. He'd forgotten how pretty she was—her grungy clothes couldn't obscure that.

"Well, I'm really glad we ran into each other." Chloe lowered her lashes and smiled at him. "You know, I had a lot of fun with you last spring. I'd love to get together again sometime—I don't really know many people on campus yet. Maybe you could show me around."

"Sure, that'd be cool. I'll give you a tour of the few decent places off campus." Tom returned her smile, feeling more at ease now. Obviously she'd just been nervous about wanting to see him again.

Girls took kisses so much more seriously than guys. Actually, it was kind of cute—an innocent freshman girl getting all skittish around him, the experienced college man. Certainly an improvement on Elizabeth's ice-queen routine.

"Great! What are you doing this Friday?" The words came out fast and breathless, the same way he used to sound asking girls out when he was in junior high. Chloe was looking cuter every minute.

"Friday's good for me. Where should I pick you up?" Tom realized too late that he probably should have hesitated longer, for the sake of creating the illusion that he might actually have plans for Friday night.

But it didn't seem to matter—Chloe looked thrilled. She was sitting up on the grass with her legs tucked under her, her head tilted at a flirtatious angle. "Would you mind meeting me at my dorm? I don't know my way around campus all that well yet."

"No problem," Tom agreed. He noticed that her whole face lit up. "Let's say seven o'clock, at . . . ?"

"Oakley Hall, wing B, room 30," Chloe said in that fast, eager voice. "I'll see you then!"

"I'm looking forward to it," Tom said, and meant it. A date with a cute freshman girl who obviously had a big crush on him was exactly what he needed right now. He waved good-bye to her and jogged up the stairs to his building, feeling rather smug. Maybe Elizabeth wouldn't care if he dropped off the face of the earth, but there were plenty of girls out there who were dying to date Wildman Watts.

"Thanks anyway," Sam said for the sixth time in five minutes. He hung up the pay-phone receiver and slashed an *X* across another of the red circles on the newspaper. He moved farther down the column, dropped another quarter into the slot, and punched in another set of numbers.

"Yeah, you're renting a room?" He wasn't bothering to put on his fake, friendly voice anymore. It was wasted effort.

The gruff man on the other end of the line apparently thought so too. "Got a deposit this morning. Ya gotta move fast, y'know—university kids're all comin' into town."

"Yep. Thanks." Sam hung up and resisted the urge to smash his fist through the phone-booth wall. Everybody felt compelled to remind him that his chances were slim, that he was an idiot and a loser to have waited until the last minute. Funny how people were always quick to tell him what he was doing wrong, when they couldn't have cared less whether he ended up all right. The only one looking out for Sam was Sam. He wished everyone else would just keep their two cents to themselves.

The phone booth felt suddenly, intensely claustrophobic. Sam slid open the door and pushed his way out, crumpling the classified ads into a ball in his hands. He got into his car, slammed the door, and peeled out of the OCC parking lot with tires screeching. He had nowhere to go, but at times like these—when he felt cornered, powerless—he knew he just had to *go*. All he could do was keep moving.

Sam sped up, vaguely soothed by the sense of motion, as he approached the on-ramp to the freeway. How had he gotten himself into this position? He hated being dependent on anyone—yet he was stuck crashing on his friends' floors indefinitely. Well, it was his own fault for not being around when they were all picking roommates and apartment hunting. Everyone Sam knew had worked out their living situations weeks ago.

Except Elizabeth. Sam veered sharply to the left and floored the accelerator. It was definitely one of fate's sick little jokes that she was his only lead on an apartment. Ninety-nine percent of his friends and acquaintances took it for granted that Sam wasn't the kind of person you tried to get close to. But Elizabeth didn't seem to understand that not everyone was secretly yearning to open up.

And worse yet, she picked up on things he thought nobody else noticed about himself.

It was stupid to even consider it. He did like her—and Jessica and Neil too. And all things being equal, he'd rather live with friends than with strangers. But Elizabeth had made it pretty clear that she would rather rent that spare room to an ax murderer than to Sam.

And even if she *was* into it, how could he live with someone who was constantly on his case? It would drive him insane to have to answer to Elizabeth all the time.

Sam gripped the steering wheel with both hands. He was crashing at his friend Mitch's place, but he had three hours to kill before Mitch came home to let him in. And not a single apartment to go see. Sam was doing sixty-five, but he felt like he was just grinding gears.

He had no options—except Elizabeth. If you could call that an option. Right now, Sam kind of felt like he had to.

At least he could see her one more time. If she'd relaxed her Sam-is-the-devil stance, fine. If not, he'd take the hint and stay out of Elizabeth's life.

"I'm starving," Dana mumbled, her breath warm on the hollow of Todd's neck. "Do we have anything to eat? And more important, can we reach it without getting up?"

They were curled together, exhausted and motionless, on the lumpy secondhand couch they had bought. The living room was dark, except for one bare bulb turning the shapes of boxes and clothing-filled trash bags into eerie shadows. It was nearly nine o'clock, and they hadn't eaten since noon. Todd's stomach was growling too, and every muscle of his body ached. He'd thought the two of them owned practically no furniture . . . until they lugged it all up those stairs.

"Can't we just get something delivered?" Todd groaned. "I think I can reach the phone from here if I *really* psych myself up for the effort."

"Well, I spent my last three dollars on getting your copies of the keys made." Dana snuggled her face closer against Todd's shoulder. "But if you've got cash, I'd love to get some sushi. Or pizza. Or . . . hmmm. Do they make pizza topped with sushi?"

"That's the most disgusting thing I've ever heard." Todd pushed an unruly lock of hair out of Dana's eyes.

"Okay, then, how about Mexican? I could go for a big old bean burrito right now. And maybe some guacamole and rice . . ."

"Mmmm . . . me too." Todd's mouth watered as his head filled with visions of a romantic dinner with Dana. But then an embarrassing realization struck him, followed instantly by a sinking sense of guilt. "Uh . . . Dana, I'm kind of tapped out too. My last fifty bucks went to the van rental."

Dana lifted her face and stared at Todd with a stricken expression. "Are you serious? We're totally broke?"

Todd swallowed hard. He should have been used to the feeling of utter inadequacy by now, but he still cringed at the awareness that he could no sooner provide Dana with dinner than he could solve world hunger. "Well," he said weakly, "my credit card might still be under the limit . . . but we'd have to drive around looking for a place that accepts it. I mean, *I* could drive around, and you could wait here," he corrected himself quickly.

In the dim light he could see Dana's wide eyes fill with tears. "I can't wait that long," she wailed. "I'm about to start gnawing cardboard boxes! Don't we have *anything* in the house?"

"I'll go look," Todd promised. He planted a quick kiss on her forehead and scrambled to his feet, his exhaustion subsumed by the urgent need to take care of Dana. "Don't worry, Dana, we'll figure out something."

He dashed to the kitchen and peered into a few cupboards but saw nothing more than mildew, matches, and a box of emergency candles. Todd rooted through a shopping bag on the counter, which, he knew, contained all the supplies Dana had grabbed hastily from her old house's kitchen. Tea bags, bouillon, nondairy creamer, nutmeg . . . not exactly stuff he could whip together into a gourmet meal. He wondered what happened to the Welcome Wagon. Weren't friendly neighbors supposed to be bringing over casseroles right about now?

Finally, at the bottom of the bag, his hands encountered a couple of cans. He pulled them out—tomato soup. Not his favorite, but at the moment they looked like prime rib.

"I found something," he called to Dana. "Where's the can opener?"

"Everything's in that box on the floor," her voice drifted back to him.

Todd rotated until he saw it. "Okay, just give me a few minutes." He rooted through the jumble of pots and pans and found the can opener, a saucepan, and some bowls. The soup directions called for milk. He briefly considered adding nondairy creamer but decided against it—water would have to do. He vowed that as soon as he had a cent to his name, he'd make this night up to Dana at a five-star restaurant.

"Todd, what's taking so long?" Dana's plaintive voice sounded from the living room as he was lighting a burner underneath the saucepan. "What are you doing in there?"

"I'm making us a romantic dinner," Todd yelled, unwrapping two newspaper-padded bundles from the box. Relief flooded through him when he saw that Dana's pair of crystal champagne flutes, a gift from her grandmother, had survived the move intact. He filled them with tap water and hurried to turn off the flame under the bubbling-over soup.

He whisked the pan off the stove and divided

171

the soup into two bowls. Then he grabbed a candle and a box of matches from the cupboard and tucked them under his arm. Carefully hugging the bowls to his chest and threading the glass stems between his fingers like he'd seen waiters do in restaurants, Todd managed to transport the entire spread to the living room.

Dana's eyes lit up when she saw him. "Oh, Todd, you actually made us a *meal!*" she exclaimed, gasping and sitting up straight on the couch. "You are, without a doubt, my favorite person in the whole, entire world. Here, let me help you with that." She took the champagne flutes from him and set them on the coffee table.

"You're right up there on my list too," Todd said, putting down the bowls on the table where Dana had just whisked away a bag of shoes. "Careful, those are hot." He wedged the candle into an empty soda can and lit it, then sat down beside Dana and lifted a glass. "Shall we toast to our first night in our new home?"

Dana lifted the other champagne flute and twined her arm with Todd's. "Here's to living in the lap of luxury." They clinked glasses and took obligatory sips of water.

Todd set down his glass and put his arms around Dana. "I know this isn't how you pictured yourself living," he said in a low voice, "but I'd rather be here with you than anywhere else."

"Me too," Dana whispered, her eyes glistening.

"And I'm going to make everything nice for you," he went on, gazing into her face so she could see how serious he was. "I'm not going to rest until I fix this place up so it's livable. Better than livable. And then I'll get a part-time job or something—whatever it takes to make sure you never, ever have to live on soup and water again. That way it'll be *me* who's taking care of you—not my parents and their bank account."

"Oh, Todd, you don't have to do all that." Dana cupped his jaw in her hands. "Just being together is enough. I love you so much."

"I love you too. . . ." His words were swallowed up by Dana's kiss. Todd returned it feverishly, his body enfolding hers in a protective embrace. If only he could hold Dana tightly enough to shut out the rest of the world.

She was gasping, her chest heaving against his, when they pulled apart. "All of a sudden I'm not fiending for soup anymore," she panted. "What do you say we christen the bedroom?"

"Don't get up," Todd said, sliding one arm under Dana's knees. "I'll carry you over the threshold."

He hoisted Dana up and brought her into the bedroom. He deposited her on the bare mattress of the futon and gave her soft lips a quick kiss. "I'll go turn out the lights. Be right back."

Todd went back to the living room, turned off the light, and blew out the candle. "I hope you're not decent," he called, hurrying back to the bedroom. "Dana?"

She was sound asleep, her mouth hanging slightly open, one arm splayed across the mattress. Todd couldn't help but smile in spite of his disappointment.

"Oh, well, we've got plenty of nights to look forward to," he whispered as he slipped Dana's shoes from her feet. He located a quilt, draped it over her, and kissed her cheek. "Sweet dreams, honey."

Chloe hovered in the hallway just outside the Oakley lounge like an actress waiting in the wings for her cue. She ran her fingers one last time through her hair to make sure it was tousled enough. Although she'd already blotted all but the last traces of her lipstick, she mashed up her mouth to ensure that her lips looked sufficiently flushed. Then she took a deep breath and sailed into the lounge as if she were floating on a cloud.

"Hey, Chloe," Eva called. "Did you just get in?" She was sitting in front of the TV with Moira, Eva, and a few freshman girls Chloe didn't know well. They all looked up when Chloe entered.

"Yeah, actually." Chloe leaned against the door frame and sighed dreamily. She faked a glance at her watch. "I can't believe how late it is!"

More like she couldn't believe how long she'd

sat in that diner booth, reading a novel, drinking way too many cups of coffee, and hoping nobody she knew would see her. But nobody *had* seen her, so her secret was safe.

"Do you mind?" Moira asked. "We're trying to watch the midnight movie."

"Where've you been all night, Chlo?" Lisa asked. "You look so nice—were you out with Tom?"

"Nice? This ancient thing?" Chloe fingered the blue vintage dress she'd agonized over, wanting to look dressed up without wearing anything expensive. "Well, thanks—Tom would *not* stop complimenting me." She smiled. "I felt like a movie star, he was paying so much attention to me."

"I wish *my* boyfriend still treated me that way," Lisa said. "He barely ever even takes me out anymore. Did you go somewhere nice?"

"El Capitano; can you believe it? It was incredible— I mean, he got the violinist to play for us and everything." Chloe hugged her arms to her chest and heaved another dreamy sigh. "Then we went out onto the dance floor . . . and you would not *believe* what an amazing dancer Tom is."

"Ohhh," Lisa wailed. "El Capitano is so expensive! I'm *so* jealous. And Jeff doesn't dance at all."

"You are *so* lucky, Chloe," Eva said.

"Believe me, I know it," Chloe agreed. Was she pushing it too far? She glanced around. Everyone looked impressed—except Moira, who was sitting rigid in front of the TV, evidently seething. "Tom's one in a million."

Chloe *was* lucky, she knew—that she could actually pull this off with a straight face. And that nothing had tripped her up so far. She had no idea what she would have done if Tom had said no today. But thankfully she didn't have to worry about that. A few hours of drinking lousy coffee in a booth was a small price to pay for perfecting the illusion. Pretty soon it would be the truth anyway.

"We should double sometime," Eva suggested. "My boyfriend would love to sit down with the famous Wildman Watts and talk football. We can totally ignore them, of course," she added.

"That sounds great," Chloe said, her smile weakening. Maybe she was getting a little ahead of herself—a lot of variables still had to add up just right to make her fantasy a reality.

"Yeah, I can't wait to meet Tom either," Lisa said. "I hear he's totally hunky."

"Only if you go for the muscular, athletic, ruggedly handsome type," Eva tittered, winking at Chloe.

"Well, you'll get your chance Friday night," Chloe told Lisa. Chloe perked up a little—what she'd just said was actually true!

"You guys, I can't hear the movie," Moira snapped without turning her head from the TV screen.

Chloe fought to keep a grin in check. Moira

was actually envious of *her*. Finally Chloe had something Moira didn't—a boyfriend.

Well, maybe she didn't *have* Tom yet. But she had a date with him. Which meant she'd already overcome the biggest hurdle. Once she was out with Tom, she'd do whatever it took to make sure he wanted to see her again. Pretty soon she wouldn't have to make up the mushy details—they'd be the truth.

But for now she'd better quit while she was ahead. Chloe feigned a wide yawn. "Well, I'm worn out from all that dancing," she said. "I'm heading off to bed."

"I might be up late," Moira said, swiveling her head just enough to glare at Chloe out of the corner of her eye. "So don't blame me if I disturb your beauty sleep."

Chloe smiled. It was almost funny to hear Moira's little jibes now that she was armed against them. "No problem." She paused in the doorway and glanced over her shoulder at her roommate. "You probably won't have to worry about tiptoeing around me at night for much longer. Did I mention Tom has a single?"

"You missed a spot," Neil said just as Jessica descended the last rung of the ladder. "Right up . . . there." He pointed to a spot inches from the living-room ceiling.

"Very funny." Jessica waved her paint roller in

his face. "How'd you like to be Neil, the yellow-nosed reindeer?"

Neil lifted his arms in surrender. "Don't make me inhale any more toxic fumes than I already have." He bent down and dipped his brush in a tray of paint. "Actually, I think we're doing a pretty styling job, if I do say so myself. I'm glad you talked me into this color."

"Me too." Jessica gazed around with satisfaction at the buttery yellow that now coated the living-room walls. "I'm not even sorry we wasted two hours picking out the trim. It was worth it."

"Picking out?" Neil snorted. "Don't you mean fighting about?" They had hotly debated the burnt-orange shade Jessica had bought for the trim—leading Elizabeth, around midnight, to throw up her hands and go to bed. Neil had taken off his watch so he wouldn't get paint all over it, but he figured it must be like two-thirty in the morning now.

"Well, whatever." Jessica dipped her roller into the tray of paint that lay on the newspaper-covered floor. "Call it what you will—I'm just glad I didn't let you talk me into that heinous puke green. It's too bad you haven't seen the new color scheme in the Theta dining room—you would've been into the orange thing right away. That place looks amazing."

"Jess, you're like a one-woman pledge drive tonight—Theta this, Theta that." Neil swirled his brush in the tray of paint. "I didn't realize you were so into your sorority. You barely mentioned it over the summer."

Jessica was a little startled. Now that she thought about it, she *had* been talking about Theta a lot all day. Slowly she rolled a shiny swath of paint across a bare patch of wall, considering how to express the sudden shift she'd experienced.

"Well," she began, "after everything that happened last year, I had mixed feelings about the Thetas. But when I went over there yesterday, I got a totally different feeling. I felt *included,* you know?"

"I guess so," Neil said. "But doesn't it bother you that you'll have to conform to certain expectations?"

Jessica shrugged. "Last year that was definitely an uphill battle. But now that my friends will be running things, I feel like I can fit in without really having to try."

"And I'm happy that you found a group you click with," Neil said as he touched up a spot by the window frame. "It's just that you're such an individual, Jess—I'd hate to see you get too caught up in *belonging* to something."

"See, that's the thing." Jessica ground her roller back and forth in the paint. "I don't want it to become my whole identity. I've been kinda wondering about how big a part of my life I want it to be."

"Well, being into your sorority doesn't mean you have to ignore all the other facets of yourself," Neil pointed out. "You don't have to let it define you."

"But what if I decide to do something like run for pledge chair?" Jessica let the roller swing down her side, spattering dots of yellow across the newspaper. "Everyone at Theta house was encouraging me, but I'm not sure I want to commit to such a big responsibility." She peeled back a paint-encrusted lock of hair that was plastered to her forehead. "What if I'm the worst pledge chair in Theta history? Or what if I run and lose? Or what if I win, but—"

"Hold up, Jess." Neil was laughing at her. "God, I never thought *you* of all people would turn out to be even more relentlessly self-scrutinizing than I am. Did it ever occur to you that maybe you could run, and win, and do a really good job, and *still* do all the other stuff you wanted to do this year?"

"Why would I think that? Elizabeth's the over-achiever, not me." Jessica couldn't keep the insecure edge out of her voice. "I'm the flighty, shallow one, remember?"

"Oh, *riiight,* I keep mixing you two up." Neil slapped his forehead. "Seriously, Jess, you have an iron will—and you're a *lot* smarter than you give yourself credit for. I bet you can do anything you put your mind to, especially if all your friends are encouraging you like you say."

180

Jessica mulled this new angle. "Maybe you're right. Maybe I shouldn't rule out anything yet." She lowered herself to the floor and stretched her weary legs in front of her, not caring if she got paint on her old sweatpants. "Throwing myself into a big responsibility could be exactly what I need right now, but maybe what will really fulfill me is something totally different."

"This is going to sound like something my mother would say about anchovies, but . . . you'll never know if you like it until you try it," Neil said.

Jessica sighed. All of a sudden she felt sapped, the hours of work catching up with her. It was so crushing to understand that there might not be a right answer—or at least not an answer *right away*.

"It's like all these decisions to make are coming at me all at once," she said. "It was agonizing enough to declare a major. I just want so badly to turn over a new leaf this year, you know? But I have no clue how to do that."

"I do know," Neil said in a low voice. "Figuring out how to move on is one of the hardest things a person can do." He frowned as he stabbed his paintbrush into the tray of paint. Then he turned to the wall, his face hidden from Jessica.

"Jeez, that sounds so serious," Jessica said, keeping a joking note in her voice. "Is there some dark secret in your past that you're trying to forget about, Neil?"

"Of course not," he answered a little too fast. He

181

turned his face to Jessica and smiled. "Wow, this room is really coming along, huh? I don't think we need another coat, do you?"

"Mmmm," Jessica responded, narrowing her eyes at Neil. Who did he think he was kidding? Jessica had practically written the book on deflection—and the sequel on abrupt subject changes. She sensed not to push it right now, but there was obviously something Neil wasn't telling her.

Chapter Ten

"Well, our one o'clock just canceled," Neil said as he hung up the kitchen phone. "He already found a place. Which means we have exactly two appointments lined up for today—and that's it for the entire rest of the week." He dropped onto the counter stool across from Jessica and Elizabeth and glared back and forth between them.

Why didn't they look half as freaked out as he felt? Didn't they care about the money they were going to lose?

"Well . . . two is better than none?" Elizabeth suggested. She was engrossed in spreading cream cheese on a bagel.

"Oh, I forgot to tell you guys—someone called while you two were at the hardware store." Jessica flipped a page of her fashion magazine. "Damian or Damon or something. He wanted to know if you found anyone for the room yet."

Neil pushed away his plate of bagel crusts, feeling his temples begin to throb. He'd woken up in a bad mood to begin with after staying up all night painting. And it rubbed him completely the wrong way that the twins refused to wake up and smell the crisis. "Jess, how could you just *forget* someone calling about the apartment? Do you realize that I have exactly three dollars and eighty-one cents in my bank account right now?"

"Chill out, Neil—we *all* want to find a housemate." Jessica took an infuriatingly nonchalant sip of her coffee and thumbed another magazine page. "I mean, I maxed out my credit card today on *textbooks,* of all things. If we don't get someone soon, I'll have to start crashing dorm events every night so I can subsist on free pizza."

"Anyway, it was just Damian," Elizabeth put in, lifting her bagel to her lips. "It's not like we want that human pincushion to move in."

Jessica snapped her fingers in recognition. "Ohhh, so that was the goth dude? Forget that—I'm not living with any guy who wears more makeup than me."

Neil ground his teeth. Maddening, just maddening. How many times did they have to have this conversation? "This isn't *The Dating Game,* okay? We don't have to *like* the person. They just have to be able to pay."

"Well, sorry," Elizabeth retorted, pausing to lean on the mop. "I thought we were in agreement that we didn't want our house used as a punk-rock recording studio."

Neil grimaced and ran his hand through his hair, too frustrated and stressed out to admit she had a point. "Well, maybe we should call some-one else back," he suggested instead. "Like the older man, Morton—so what if he's not the most with-it guy? I'm sure he'd make a perfectly fine housemate."

Jessica made a pouty-little-girl face as she set down her mug of coffee on the counter. "Can't we just wait a few more days? Maybe we'll find a young, *cute* guy."

Neil closed his eyes and squeezed the bridge of his nose between his fingertips. "Could you please take this seriously, Jess? The *stupidest* thing we could do is move in someone that one of us is attracted to."

"Neil's right," Elizabeth said so suddenly that Neil cast a wary glance in her direction. She caught his eye and then lowered her gaze, biting into her bagel.

"Well, whatever," Neil said. "The point is, Jess, we don't have a few days. At least, *I* don't. If we hold off much longer, we can't expect anyone to pay us back for this month's rent."

"So what do you want me to do about it?" Jessica was beginning to look upset. "I'm nervous too, but it's not like I can just produce a house-mate from up my sleeve—cute or not. I mean, we already put up flyers everywhere. If nobody's interested, what can we do?"

Elizabeth was strangely silent, munching her bagel and staring into space. Either she was holding something back, or she didn't want to get involved in another argument. Neil was about to snipe at her when he realized how weary he was of bickering with the twins. Trying to convey his stress level to them only got him more worked up.

"Well, I guess we'd better hope one of these two appointments today works out," Neil said. "If not . . ." He trailed off, leaving the thought unfinished. *If not, the two of you are on your own.* He couldn't constantly be goading them into action when he had his own life to worry about. Maybe he couldn't afford his own place, but there were always roommate searches or even youth hostels. If the twins were unwilling or unable to take any initiative in finding a housemate, he'd have to take the initiative himself—and start looking for somewhere else to live.

"I come bearing snack foods!" Todd announced as he nudged open the kitchen door with his foot, then used his shoulder to open it farther. He barged in, arms full of groceries, and set the overflowing bags on the counter. "I got everything that could possibly rot our teeth or clog our arteries, plus some healthy stuff too—just in case we get a craving or something."

186

Dana was crouched on the floor, her head and shoulders lost inside a cabinet under the sink. She didn't even turn around when Todd came in. "Thanks," her voice called from somewhere inside the cabinet. "Did you pick up some cleanser and steel wool like I asked?"

"Yeah. They're right here." Todd felt a little disappointed as he lifted the cleaning products out of a bag. The least Dana could do was sound a little more excited. He'd hated going to the bank to withdraw another chunk of the money his parents set up for him—what kind of man lived on Mommy and Daddy's money? And then he'd driven around for twenty minutes before he could find a grocery store. He'd spent two hours comparing prices, clipping coupons, and wondering if generic brands were the same as real brands, and here Dana was, barely approving that he'd remembered the cleaning products.

"Great. This kitchen is so filthy, I think the mildew's been running the show for the last twenty years." Dana extracted herself from the cabinet, a completely blackened sponge in her hand, and straightened up. Her hair was wrapped in a kerchief, her arms were covered up to the elbows by yellow rubber gloves, and there was a smudge of something oily on one cheek. Todd thought she looked adorable.

"Hey, not so fast." He moved toward her, tilting his face for a kiss, as Dana reached for the cleanser. "Aren't you going to tip the delivery boy?"

Dana ducked her head away. "Don't touch me right now. I'm totally disgusting." She grabbed the cleanser and disappeared back inside the cabinet, her shoulder blades straining back and forth as she scrubbed in long strokes.

Todd stood there awkwardly for a second, then busied himself with unpacking the grocery bags. He knew Dana was harried, trying to make the apartment livable, but he couldn't help feeling rejected. Since when had they ever let a little thing like personal hygiene stand in the way of a kiss?

He tried again. "Hey, when we're finished with the kitchen, want to take a ride to campus? Tomorrow's the deadline for registration, you know—I thought we could get all our paperwork and everything taken care of, then maybe go out for a nice dinner." It would have to be courtesy of his parents' money, but Todd vowed to get a part-time job soon. He had to start living like an adult.

He opened the refrigerator and put a carton of milk on the shelf, keeping the corner of his eye on Dana.

"I don't think I'm *ever* going to be done with this kitchen." Dana eased herself out of the cabinet and plopped down on the floor as if all the energy had drained out of her. "It took me all morning just to clean the oven, and I'm only halfway through the cabinets." Just then, she

188

seemed to register what he was doing, and she sucked in her breath in alarm. "You're not putting food in that bacteria-infested fridge, are you? Take it out right now! That milk's probably already curdled from all the germs in there!"

"Okay, okay—you don't have to yell." Todd withdrew the carton of milk and sullenly picked a sponge from the open package on the counter.

"Well, *sorry,* but I thought it would be obvious when you looked in the fridge that you wouldn't put fresh food in there before I cleaned it." Dana slammed the cabinet door shut and got up to rinse her sponge out in the sink.

"Hard to find good help these days, isn't it?" Todd deadpanned through gritted teeth. He rolled up his sleeves and started scrubbing the inside of the refrigerator. Now that he looked closely, it really was grimy—but still, that was no reason for Dana to start nagging at him like she was his mother. Their little love nest was seeming less romantic by the second.

After a few tense minutes of silence Todd was desperate to fill the air. "So when do you want to register?" he persisted, sidling to the sink to rinse out the sponge. "Don't you think tomorrow's cutting it a little close? We'll have to deal with the crunch of everyone else who waited until the last minute."

Dana sighed heavily as she opened the door of another cabinet. "Just dealing with this apartment

189

is like a full-time commitment. I don't know when I'm going to have time to get to campus and wait on endless lines at the registrar's. There's a lot to do here, stuff I *want* to do. I'm not sure I'll even register at all."

Todd paused, sponge in midwring, and blinked at Dana. "So what are you saying? That you've all of a sudden decided to drop out of school?"

He expected her to say *of course not*. But Dana shrugged. "I don't know. I haven't thought it out that far. All I know is that classes and papers and exams are like the *last* thing on my mind right now. I can't see myself snapping back into that mind-set."

"But what about your cello? What about . . ." Todd lapsed into helpless silence. He didn't even know where to begin. This was totally out of left field. Dana must be even more stressed out than Todd imagined to consider not registering for the semester.

"Listen, don't worry about it. I was only thinking out loud, not making a plan, okay?" Dana turned to the cabinet and bore down with some steel wool in frantic circles. "I just wasn't counting on having to deal with moving, and doing all this cleaning, and being strapped for cash. It's a lot to take on when you're a full-time student."

Todd winced as he turned back to the fridge. Obviously Dana still resented him for messing up her life—not that he could blame her. He was beginning to worry that he'd been naive to think he could make everything all right by finding them a place. Already they were squabbling over household chores like an old married couple. Maybe all this responsibility, all this commitment, was too much pressure for a couple to handle—even one as strong as they were.

He gazed over at Dana, who was vigorously scrubbing out the cabinet, her back to him. Just days ago they couldn't keep their hands off each other, and now she would rather get up close and personal with dust and mold than kiss him.

Todd felt his heart constrict. Maybe living together *was* too much too soon. Maybe taking the plunge into serious couplehood had backfired. In signing that lease, he might very well have signed the death warrant for the best relationship he'd ever had.

"Liz, could you get that?" Jessica asked over the shrilling phone. She screwed the cap onto a bottle of dark brown polish and set it on the coffee table. "My nails still aren't totally dry yet."

"What am I, the maid?" Elizabeth snapped across the cotton-ball-strewn coffee table, lowering the arts course catalog she was poring over. "Get it yourself." She was still irritated with her sister after the borderline-rude disinterest with which Jessica had treated their first roommate interview, a geeky science major. (Okay, so they would have ruled him out anyway after he swore up and down that his chemistry experiments rarely resulted in explosions. But Jessica hadn't known that when she snubbed him at first sight.)

"Come *on*, Liz, don't make me mess up the final coat—I'll have to start all over," Jessica begged, shaking out her hands in front of her as the phone continued to bleat. "Anyway, you're like a foot farther away from it than I am. What's the big deal?"

The big deal, although Elizabeth wasn't about to spell it out, was simply that tensions in the duplex had been mounting since their housemate conversation that morning. Both candidates they'd seen were total washouts—the second girl was adamant about bringing her two cats, and Neil was violently allergic. The situation was beginning to look desperate. They had even called Morton back, but he'd already found a place.

"What would you do if I *wasn't* around?" Elizabeth challenged. She knew she was just taking out her frustration on her twin, but she couldn't help herself. "You'd better start learning to do things for yourself, Jess!"

Jessica looked up from blowing on her fingertips. "You know, I'm getting pretty darn sick of—"

"*I'll* get the damn phone!" Neil barked, emerging from the kitchen and lunging for the receiver. "Hello!"

His voice softened instantly. "Oh, hey, Sam!"

Elizabeth's whole body tensed. She felt her throat close up as if she had just swallowed a cork.

"Hey, long time no see . . . yeah, you too! How did you get this number anyway?" Neil's face dropped into an expression of pure shock. "You did? Oh, she *did*, did she?" He turned narrow, slitted eyes on Elizabeth. "No, she never mentioned it."

Elizabeth swallowed hard and averted her eyes.

Jessica was looking back and forth between Neil and Elizabeth. "Liz, what's up?" she asked.

Elizabeth, straining to make out the conversation, shook her head and waved her hands in an I'll-explain-later gesture.

"You're still . . . what? . . . Oh, about the room!" Neil slapped his forehead. "Great! See, we never knew you were ever interested in the first place." Neil's tone was friendly, but Elizabeth could sense the unspoken outrage that was directed at her. She wondered if anyone would notice if she crawled under the chair to hide.

"Yeah, we'd love that! Just like old times, right?" Neil grinned at something Sam was saying. "Remember that night . . . Yeah, yeah, that's the one!" Neil listened for a second, then threw back his head and exploded into laughter. "Stop, man, you're killing me!" he wheezed. "Oh, that's too funny."

Elizabeth clenched her jaw and rolled her eyes. Typical. Sam was always at his most charming when he wanted something.

"Sounds great. We'll see you then." Another hearty laugh. "I hear you. Okay, take it easy." Neil replaced the receiver. "So Sam's stopping by tonight to check out the room," he explained. "If he likes it, and if nobody has any objections"—he glanced at Elizabeth—"he's willing to write us a check on the spot and move in tomorrow."

"Great news!" Jessica clapped. "Wow, actually living with someone we know—that would be so perfect!"

"You'd think that, wouldn't you? But apparently *someone* didn't see it that way." Neil turned blazing eyes on Elizabeth. "You know, we could have saved a lot of time and stress if we'd known that a friend of ours was looking for a place. Liz, why the hell didn't you tell us Sam was interested?"

Elizabeth gulped, suppressing the urge to point out that it had been Neil who said they shouldn't rent to a person who one of them was attracted to. There was no need to bring *that* into it. "He's a jerk," she replied instead. "He constantly gets on my nerves, and there's no way I could live under the same roof with him."

"Come on, Liz, you're exaggerating," Jessica argued. "You and Sam had your clashes this summer, but so did we all. At least he's a known quantity—we can be pretty sure he's not going to start playing industrial music late at night or blow up the building with some science experiment."

194

"But—But how can we be sure he'll even pay his rent?" Elizabeth stammered. "I mean, he's totally unreliable, and . . ." She trailed off, cowering before Jessica and Neil's skeptical expressions. She was grasping at straws, and it was obvious they knew it.

"Listen, Liz, ever since we got here, you've been lecturing me about growing up and taking responsibility and blah, blah, blah." Jessica jabbed a freshly painted fingertip accusingly at Elizabeth. "Well, you have to act like a grown-up too! If it were *me* who was being irrational about not living with a perfectly normal person, *you'd* go ballistic!"

Elizabeth opened her mouth to protest and promptly realized she had no leg to stand on. It was true: If the situation were reversed, she'd be calling Jessica selfish and immature. The whole time, the three of them had been wishing they could live with a friend instead of a stranger. She couldn't justify being opposed to Sam moving in . . . unless she brought up the extenuating circumstances that she very much didn't want to mention.

"Okay, I'm totally busted," Elizabeth admitted. "If Sam wants to move in and you guys want him here, I'll be big enough to deal."

Nina swept her pink highlighter across the ruler-lined grid she had drawn on graph paper, being careful to stay inside the lines that demarcated three to five P.M. Pink was for physics, Monday through Friday. She picked up her pencil and lightly cross-hatched the Tuesday and Thursday boxes to mark the fact that those days were labs, not lectures. She consulted her registration printout, then took the blue highlighter—blue for biology—and colored in nine to eleven A.M. on Monday and Wednesday.

"Who says I don't know how to have a good time?" she muttered to herself as she tacked the completed schedule on the bulletin board above her desk.

Nina leaned back in her desk chair and contemplated the squares that represented every day of every week of this semester. The bright patchwork jumble of colors blurred before her into one endless block of drudgery. She was already starting to feel overwhelmed by work, even though she hadn't been assigned any yet. Staring at the rare slivers of blank space on her schedule, she had the sinking realization that she could look forward to many more wild nights like this one.

She rubbed her tired eyes. Was this what people meant when they said youth was wasted on the young? Nina had the feeling that people in retirement homes led more exciting lives than hers.

Nina got up and paced her dorm room like a caged animal. "Why did I register for all those classes anyway?" She groaned aloud.

Of course, she knew why—because she'd somehow thought that being saddled with a hellish workload would distract her from thoughts of Bryan. But now the thought of all those classes just seemed oppressive. It wasn't like she required free time to be depressed about Bryan—memories of him seeped into her consciousness no matter what she was doing. Now she wondered if she wouldn't have been better off giving herself some time to breathe.

Nina sat down on her bed and dropped her head into her hands. Her world seemed to be closing in around her, rapidly shrinking to the size of her desk. Already she felt like she was barely holding herself together, and yet she had gone ahead and created more stress in her life. Why was she always so hard on herself? Other people managed to draw the line between being ambitious and being masochistic.

A bloodcurdling scream from somewhere just outside her door startled her out of her funk. Nina was on her feet before she was aware of having reacted. "Shondra?" she called.

Another scream. Nina bolted out of her room and into the common area. It was empty. Her roommate's door was closed. Everything was silent.

"Shondra, are you okay?" Nina called.

An instant later there was an anguished wail from inside Shondra's room, barely muffled by the door. Then a stream of curses, so fast and furious it was unintelligible. "You *dog*," Shondra's voice screeched. "You pig! You filthy, disgusting, sickening *pig!*"

Her heart knocking against her windpipe, Nina noticed that the phone cord snaked under Shondra's door. She saw it go taut, then relax, then go taut again, as if Shondra were pacing around with the receiver. *Kendrick?* Nina wondered. She wouldn't have pegged her roommate to have such violent arguments with her boyfriend.

"You make me sick," Shondra half sobbed, half spat. "How could you do this to me? How *could* you? I hate you, I hate you, I hate you!" The words were punctuated by a crash and the sound of something shattering. Nina guessed it was one of the many photos in the Kendrick shrine. Then came the softer sound of weeping.

Nina hovered by the door, holding her arms. She wondered if it was her place to intrude. Obviously this was a horribly painful moment for Shondra. But then, Nina knew exactly what her suite mate was going through—the scene with Bryan and that skank was flashing through her mind as vividly as if it were yesterday. Maybe Shondra needed someone to open up to as much as Nina did. If Nina reached out to her suite mate now, it could turn into a bonding experience. Tentatively Nina knocked on the door.

There was another vicious explosion of curses. Then Shondra screamed, "*Go away!* Leave me the hell alone!"

Nina took that as a no on the bonding thing. Terrified, she hurried back to her room as more crashes and bangs emanated from Shondra's room. She shut the door behind her and locked it. It looked like she was going to be spending even more time alone in her room than she'd thought.

"Darling, this is the best dinner I've ever tasted. How did you find time to do all this and still fix up the house?"

Dana stared as the attractive young power couple on TV kissed over plates of an artfully arranged appetizer. She and Todd were sitting side by side on the couch, eating macaroni and cheese with ketchup off paper plates and watching a law drama on one of the two stations her ancient color TV picked up. "How *do* people find the time to live like that? After two hours in that registration line today, it was all I could do to mix the sauce packet with the milk."

"They don't," Todd answered in a monotone, hunched over his plate. "It's just TV, Dana. Real people either get takeout or, if they're rich enough, they have servants who do everything for them."

Dana gazed at the business-suited woman fingering her pearls on-screen. It seemed like every time Dana tried to talk to Todd today, she got shot down. Something was eating away at him, but obviously he would rather hold it inside than talk to her about it.

"How was your day, darling?" Young Power Woman was asking her chiseled-jawed counterpart, leaning forward with her chin on her hands to hang on every word.

Dana set down her bowl of noodles on the coffee table. "So, uh, are you happy with the classes you registered for?" she asked, turning attentively to Todd.

He shrugged. "I guess I didn't give it much thought. I declared a business major because . . . well, I had to pick something." He cleared his throat awkwardly. "What about you? Are you glad you decided to stay in school?"

Normally Dana would have baby-voiced a "yes, sweetie, you were so right" and then snuggled next to him for a big kiss. But the vibe between them was so strained and unnatural that she didn't know what to say or do. She took a chance on joking back. "Of course! My chances of getting a good job will be *much* better if I have a music degree! Do you have any idea how marketable the cello is?"

It was the wrong call. Todd looked offended. He set down his bowl of noodles and stared at her. "Dana, what happened? I thought the cello was your passion. But ever since we moved in here, you're talking like you want to give up. Do you have any idea how terrible I'll feel if you blow off your life's dream because I made you move to this apartment?"

Frustration billowed up in Dana. His logic was so wrong, she didn't even know where to begin. "Todd, this isn't about you, and it's not about my dreams. I just have to figure out how to balance—"

"How can you say this isn't about me?" Todd cut her off. "It hurts me more than you know to see how unhappy you are . . . and to know that none of this would have happened if I hadn't gotten you kicked out of your place!" He ran his hands through his hair.

"Todd, just because I'm having a hard time doesn't mean I'm *blaming* you." Dana took him by the shoulders and gazed into his eyes. "And I don't want you to blame yourself! You just have to accept that it's going to be rough adjusting to living together."

"But it's like you don't even *want* to adjust," Todd said. "You keep talking like you don't think we can handle school and living here. What do you really want, Dana?"

"I *do* want this," Dana insisted. "It's just scary to think about going to school and still finding a way to make a life together in this apartment. I mean, I know it's *not* as easy as it looks on TV." Dana gestured at the couple on the screen. "But we can do this, I swear! We just have to work really hard."

She reached for his hand, but Todd stiffened and pulled away. "Just one question: When did being together turn into *work?*"

"Todd, you're not listening!" Dana cried in desperation.

"Well, you're not saying anything I want to hear." He gave her a long, charged look. She could see the pain and confusion in his eyes, but she had no idea what it would take to get through to him.

After a moment Todd shot up off the couch, stalked through the bedroom door, and slammed it shut.

Left alone in the silence, Dana became aware that the power couple on TV had tossed the dishes aside and were kissing passionately on the dining-room table. Dana covered her face with her hands and burst into tears.

Why couldn't Todd see that she needed him to support her . . . that it did them no good for him to feel guilty and defensive? They were both scared, both a little lost. Somehow she had to make him see that they were in this together—or they might not get through it at all.

"Well, here it is." Elizabeth flicked on the light switch and flattened herself against the wall of the downstairs bedroom, arms folded across her chest. "Not exactly deluxe accommodations."

"Oh, it's not so bad." Sam scanned the room,

maintaining a poker face to pretend he didn't notice Elizabeth's none-too-subtle attempts to discourage him. Neil was his usual friendly self, and Jessica was as effusive as ever, but Elizabeth had been giving him the deep-freeze treatment since he arrived at the duplex. He was doing his best to smooth things over for the sake of the living situation, but evidently Elizabeth wasn't having it.

"It's pretty small," Elizabeth pointed out, her intentions transparent through her innocent aren't-I-helpful tone. "And keep in mind, it might get kind of noisy living next to the kitchen."

From the corner of his eye Sam saw Jessica elbow Elizabeth in the ribs. He suppressed the urge to laugh.

"Actually, it's not bad at all," he said, picturing his few belongings arrayed in the room. It *was* a little on the small side, but he didn't exactly have a lot of stuff—Sam wasn't the type of person who attached sentimental value to objects. "Is there a back door too or just the front?"

"Well, the backyard is through the kitchen," Jessica explained, "so that sort of counts as a back door, although you'd have to hop the fence to get in or out of the yard. Perfect for sneaking in past curfew . . . you *do* know Elizabeth makes us come home promptly at midnight, right?"

Sam might have taken her seriously if Neil hadn't snickered. Elizabeth stared daggers at her twin, but Jessica merely rolled her eyes. "Oh, relax, Liz, it was just a joke. You've been hyper-uptight all day."

Elizabeth looked so uncomfortable that Sam would have felt bad for her . . . if he hadn't known it was *him* she was uptight about. "Anyway," he went on, sidestepping the awkwardness, "I asked about the door because I'm out late a lot. Other than that, I'm an ideal housemate—if I do say so myself. So this is perfect, that I can come in and out through the kitchen without disturbing you."

"With a different girl every night, you mean," Elizabeth muttered under her breath, just loud enough for Sam to hear. He let the comment roll off him—he'd have to get used to doing that if they were going to make this work. Hopefully a couple weeks of good behavior would be all it took to get Elizabeth to ease up and realize he wasn't so bad.

"Well, I'm a night person myself," Neil said, "so I'm sure we won't have a problem."

"Same here—I'd be more worried if you were planning on waking up at six A.M. for push-ups and stomach crunches." Jessica shuddered. "People like that scare me. Besides, our bedrooms are all upstairs anyway, so it's not like we'd really hear you. So, are you saying you'll take the room?"

He cast a wary glance at Elizabeth and saw her watching him anxiously, her lips pinched together. He wanted to give her a truce-declaring smile, but she looked away when he caught her eye.

Sam turned back to Jessica and pulled his checkbook from his back jeans pocket. "I'd love to," he said, clicking the cap on his pen. "Who should I make this out to?"

"Oh, let Neil have it—he's practically got dollar signs in his eyes right now," Jessica said, punching Neil on the arm.

"Hey, just because I had to count pennies to get a dry bagel this morning," Neil protested. "I will take that check, though."

"Don't spend it all in one place." Sam tore off the check and handed it to Neil with a flourish. He was aware that Elizabeth remained coldly silent.

"Thanks, man." Neil folded up the check and put it in the pocket of his navy crew-neck T-shirt. "I'll cash this today, and I promise not to flee the country."

"Yay, we have a new housemate!" Jessica cheered, giving Sam a quick hug. "Come on, let's get out of this shoe box—kidding!—and celebrate with some tap water and saltines."

"Mmmm, saltines." Neil filed out into the kitchen after Jessica. Elizabeth turned to follow, but Sam tugged at the sleeve of her cardigan.

"Wakefield, can I talk to you a second?" He nudged the door shut with his foot. "I know I'm not your idea of a dream housemate, but we're going to have to figure out a way to get along.

And I . . ." He took a deep breath. It was so difficult for him to be forthcoming about anything approaching a genuine feeling. But he had to make the attempt unless he wanted to live in a permanent war zone with Elizabeth.

She was looking up at him, half expectant, half skeptical. He summoned up all his best intentions. "I just want you to know that I'm willing to do whatever it takes to make this work . . . if you're willing to overlook the fact that I'm the worst guy you've ever met."

Elizabeth couldn't meet his eyes, but the faintest vestiges of a smile touched her pink face. "Well, maybe not *the* worst," she allowed.

She was warming up. Sam relaxed a little. "All I'm saying, Liz," he went on, "is don't make this harder than it has to be. I mean, give me a little credit—girls every night?" He flashed her his most winning grin. "We're talking every *other* night, maximum."

Elizabeth's face dropped, and she rolled her eyes. "You're so obnoxious." She extracted her arm from his grasp and turned to head out of the room.

Sam scowled at her retreating back. Fine—he tried. If she wasn't going to meet him halfway, there was no point in putting forth an effort to compromise. No more walking on eggshells around Elizabeth, no more censoring himself to appease her. From now on he was just going to be his normal *obnoxious* self.

*   *   *

"I'm not crazy! You're the crazy one!" A crash, a thump, then a smash. "I hate you! You can drop dead for all I care!"

Nina sat huddled on her bed, arms around her knees, in a state of something like shell shock. At first her heart had gone out to Shondra, but now Nina's skin was crawling with fear. It had been hours, and the torrent of rage from her suite mate's room showed no sign of letting up.

"Well, I never want to see you again as long as I live!" The door was flung open, and Shondra's shrieks came closer. "I wish I'd never met you!"

Nina squeezed her eyes shut and tried to calm her nerves with deep breaths. She had abandoned all pretense of trying to read or listen to music; she couldn't blot out the racket that whirled nearer and farther away like a tornado. From what she'd managed to gather, Kendrick had indeed dumped Shondra—and her reaction made Nina's breakup tirade at Bryan sound like a letter of recommendation.

"Good! Fine! Good-bye—forever!" Shondra let out a strangled animal cry. Then came the jingling crash of the phone being dashed to the floor. Footsteps thundered across the room, and then a door—Nina thought it was the front—slammed shut so hard that the walls vibrated.

When the hum died down, the room was eerily silent except for a faint dial tone. Nina uncurled her limbs and slipped off the bed, heart pounding.

What if Shondra wasn't really gone? She tiptoed to the door and pressed her ear against it but heard no signs of movement.

Timidly Nina cracked open the door and peered out. In an instant the bottom of her stomach dropped out. She let the door swing open and stood gaping.

The entire common room had been trashed. Nina's refrigerator lay open on its side, a carton of orange juice pooling on the carpet. Her portable stereo had been knocked almost to the other side of the room. Picture frames—Nina's as well as Shondra's—lay in shards on the floor, along with partially shattered cassette tapes. Nina's physics books were strewn everywhere, some soaked in the spilled juice. The can of daisies had been thrown across the room, leaving a streaky trail of water down the wall and a wet tangle of trampled flowers on the floor. The open door to Shondra's room revealed a similar scene of devastation.

Nina's whole body was limp. She felt like she was going to be sick.

Half her belongings were ruined. But that was the least of her worries. She was living with someone who was actually capable of this. In all the depths of her despair and anger at Bryan, Nina could never imagine losing control so completely.

Unable to bear looking at the damage any longer, Nina shut her door and shuffled back into her room. She dropped onto the bed like a dead weight and burst into tears. Before, her problems had already seemed immense. Now she didn't even feel safe in her own room. She couldn't stay here and live with a psychopath. What was she going to do?

Elizabeth had lathered her hair full of conditioner and piled it on top of her head. She filled her bath sponge full of body wash and covered herself in soapy foam—and then heard the faint but unmistakable sound of the doorbell.

"Jess!" Elizabeth screeched, her eyes squeezed shut to keep out the conditioner trickling down her forehead. But there was no sound over the rush of the shower. Of course—it was only nine-thirty, and Jessica could sleep through an earthquake. Neil had gone out first thing to cash Sam's check, and it was probably him ringing the bell because he forgot his key.

"Coming!" she shouted, hurrying to rinse her hair and body. She turned off the water and grabbed a towel off the rack.

After barreling down the stairs, she flung open the front door and gasped. Sam was standing there with a guy in a baseball cap, both carrying cardboard boxes. Instantly Elizabeth felt her face flame. She was excruciatingly conscious of the fact that all she had on was a towel—a towel that barely skimmed her knees.

"Whoa," the guy in the cap whispered, his eyes not quite reaching Elizabeth's face. "Sam, can I come visit you here? A lot?"

"Just ignore Floyd." Sam flashed his crooked grin. "This is Floyd. Floyd, this is, uh . . . Jess?"

"Elizabeth!" she snapped. That was really adding insult to injury.

"Sorry. It's hard to tell with no clues." Sam shifted the weight of the box he was carrying. "So, not to be rude, but are you going to let us in? This is kind of heavy."

Elizabeth held open the door, keeping one hand on the spot where her towel was fastened. Rivulets of water streamed from the locks of hair that were plastered to her bare shoulders. She glared at Sam. "You're an hour and a half early."

"Yeah, well, Floyd wanted to get an early start. And I couldn't move the futon frame without his van." Sam strode past her as he talked, setting the box down on the floor. Elizabeth had to work very hard to ignore the way his biceps rippled under his white T-shirt.

"It's a pleasure to meet you, and may I say that I *really* like your outfit." Floyd put down his box and stuck out his hand to Elizabeth. She gave him a look that hopefully conveyed her opinion of stupid comments like that one, and he dropped his arm to his side.

"Oh, Liz," Sam said. "With all this moving I've really worked up a sweat. Could I borrow your towel for a second?"

Floyd erupted into laughter. Sam grinned. Elizabeth seethed. She was dying to tell Sam off, but there was no way she would stoop to his level—especially not in a towel. She turned and marched up the stairs.

"I'll be in my room," Elizabeth huffed over her shoulder. "For a long, long time."

The door to room 30 at Oakley Hall cracked open a sliver, and a pale, dark-haired girl trained green, catlike eyes on Tom. "And you are?"

"Hi, I'm here to see Chloe?" He smiled. "I'm Tom Watts."

The girl arched her eyebrows. "So you *do* exist."

"Looks that way." Tom laughed nervously. What the hell was that supposed to mean?

The girl swung the door open all the way, and Tom was startled to see Chloe flanked by three other girls, all of whom were staring excitedly at Tom as if they'd been expecting him. "Uh . . . hi," he said, plastering on a polite smile.

"Hi, Tom!" Chloe stepped forward, smiling.

"These are a few of my floor mates. They were just . . . helping me get ready."

"Well, you look great," Tom said. It was true, though—she cleaned up pretty nicely. Her short black spaghetti-strap dress revealed slender curves that had been hidden under her baggy clothes the other day. Rhinestone bobby pins swept her auburn hair off her shoulders.

A blond girl beside Chloe clasped her hands and sighed. "Oh, you two look sooo cute together! Can we take a picture of you?"

Tom smiled uncomfortably. Chloe laughed. "Oh, stop, Lisa."

"So where are you two headed tonight?" A dark-haired girl who looked vaguely familiar—a friend of Winston and Denise's, maybe?—was smiling at him.

"Oh, well, I thought we'd go to, uh, Gurulé's—they have great Mexican—and then maybe for a drink at Starlights," Tom said.

"Ohhh, romantic," the girl cooed. "That's *so* great!"

"Um . . . thanks." Now Tom was distinctly ill at ease. He hadn't been thinking of this as a particularly *romantic* night so much as showing Chloe around town. Sure, they'd kissed once, but that was months ago. So why were Chloe's friends hovering around like parents seeing their daughter off to the prom?

"You must be looking forward to a nice night

out, after putting in all those hours of practice," said a tall girl with dark, short hair like Cleopatra's. "Chloe's been telling us all about how you're back on the team."

"Oh, she has?" Tom looked at Chloe, who grinned a little sheepishly. Now it made sense—she'd been bragging about having a date with him because he was on the team. Of course. All the attention was starting all over again.

Tom couldn't help puffing up a bit with pride. The other girls were gazing dreamily at him and Chloe—even the one who'd answered the door had relaxed her poker face into a wistful half smile.

"Well, we'd better get going, hon," Chloe said. At least that was what Tom *thought* she said. Could she really be calling him pet names? That would be jumping the gun, to say the least. Maybe she'd just said *huh*.

"Great." Tom helped Chloe on with her tiny cardigan sweater. When she had shrugged both arms into the sleeves, she turned to face him . . . and leaned in toward his lips. Before Tom had time to register what was happening, they were tangled in an intense embrace, mouths locked in a fiery kiss that was *way* more intense than anything he would expect from a second date. It was unexpected and a little unsettling—but he certainly wasn't complaining.

When she finally broke away from him, Chloe's

features were flushed pink. "Well, we're off," she said breathlessly. Then she turned to the cat-eyed girl and said, "Don't wait up."

Elizabeth placed her grandmother's silver candlesticks on the square of lace covering the surface of her dresser. A smile of satisfaction spread across her face as she stepped back to admire her handiwork. Her room was really starting to take shape—to feel like *her* space.

Around the perimeter of the low ceiling she had strung a length of silver tinsel stars. From the apex of the roof hung a ceramic angel, a Christmas ornament Jessica had given her. With the gauzy, sky blue curtains and the mosslike, pale green carpet, the room had a kind of fairy-tale charm, an enchanted quality.

"Maybe I really *will* feel inspired here," Elizabeth murmured. The room certainly didn't seem like a starving writer's garret anymore.

Suddenly she was glad she had drawn the short straw. There was something special about this room, now that she'd taken the time to make her mark on it. It really felt like a refuge, a peaceful place to collect her thoughts and maybe put them into writing. For the first time since she'd moved in, Elizabeth truly felt excited about having a place to call her own.

An impossibly loud burst of hip-hop music shattered the silence—beat throbbing, bass pumped up so high, the floor practically trembled.

"What the . . ." Elizabeth ventured down the stairs toward the noise. If it was this loud up in the attic, she couldn't fathom what it must be like downstairs.

She hurried to the living room, plugging her ears with her fingers, and found Sam and Floyd blasting the stereo at a volume Elizabeth hadn't thought it was capable of. The empty beer cans that littered the coffee table were actually vibrating from the noise. Sam and Floyd, their backs to Elizabeth, were intently bent over something.

"Turn down the music!" Elizabeth bellowed at the top of her lungs.

Sam turned, registered her presence, and reached out to turn down the stereo a hair. "What? Did you say something, Wakefield?"

Elizabeth ground her teeth. "I said turn the music *down!*"

"Sorry, Grandma." Sam snorted. He turned the volume knob to a level that was still outside what Elizabeth considered an acceptable range but at least didn't make her worry that her eardrums would start bleeding. She heaved a sigh of relief and was about to head back to her room when she caught a glimpse of what Sam and Floyd were so engrossed in.

Elizabeth stared, aghast. "What is *that?*"

Sam straightened up and flashed his lopsided

grin. *"That,"* he said, "is my prize possession—my collection of beer cans from around the world." He spread out his arms like a game-show host, indicating the three-foot-high aluminum eyesore that loomed over the room.

"And *what*," Elizabeth sputtered, fists clenched in fury, "is it doing in my living room?"

"We're forming 'em into a pyramid," Floyd explained, setting a can on the top tier.

"No biggie." Sam's cocky smile was maddening. "Just putting my own touches on *our* living room."

"It is a . . . a biggie!" Elizabeth exclaimed. Every second she noticed something else horribly unsightly about the beer-can pyramid—like that she was pretty sure she saw mold on a few tiers. And it was against the back wall, where it would be the first thing anyone saw when they entered the room from outside or came down from upstairs. "I am not about to stand here and let you clutter up our common space with a big pile of garbage!"

"Garbage? Show some respect!" It was hard to tell if Sam was actually indignant or just mocking her tone. "It took me years to amass these. Some of them I brought back all the way from Mexico!" He held up a red can marked *Cerveza* and placed it on the pyramid.

"How enterprising of you," Elizabeth said. She couldn't believe she was having this conversation.

It was like Sam had somehow managed to regress even further back into adolescence. "Well, you can either move it to your room as a constant reminder of your adventures in international bar hopping or I'm putting it out with the recycling tomorrow!"

"Oh, c'mon, cutie, don't be such a buzz kill," Floyd protested. "This place needs more of a guy vibe. I haven't seen such a girly room since my little sister gave her Barbie Dream House to Goodwill. I mean, look at these curtains!" He gestured at the orange crushed-velvet drapes.

"What's wrong with the curtains?"

Elizabeth whirled to see Neil standing behind her, an irate expression on his face. "I come out here to see what all the noise is about and find some random jerk in *my* house insulting the curtains *I* picked out?"

"Yo, Neil, that's my friend," Sam said.

Floyd's jaw dropped. "A *guy* picked out those curtains?"

Sam gave Floyd a warning look. "I'm not putting down your decor," he told Neil. "I just want a chance to put some of my stuff in here too."

"What stu—oh my God!" Neil's eyes bulged, obviously registering the beer-can pyramid for the first time. "You're not actually planning on keeping that monstrosity in here? That thing is a planned community for cockroaches!"

Elizabeth exhaled in relief. Thank goodness she had an ally in Neil. Now that Sam was outvoted, they could put a stop to this insanity.

But Sam's arms were folded across his chest in an utterly uncompromising stance. "Not everybody's into the house-beautiful thing, you know. I'm not into your aesthetic either, but I have to deal with it—so *you* have to deal with mine!"

"Do you want anything while I'm up?" Dana called from the kitchen.

"No, thanks." Todd was sprawled on the couch, his eyes glued to the baseball game on TV, a can of beer perched on his T-shirted stomach. The realization hit him with horrifying force—in the space of two days, he and Dana had become his parents.

Dana appeared in the living room. "Hey, will it bother you if I practice my cello for a while? I'll go in the bedroom so I don't disturb you too much."

Great. The last thing his frayed nerves needed was some whiny, high-pitched scraping. It hadn't even occurred to him that Dana would be practicing her cello in the apartment. Yet more proof that he hadn't given nearly enough thought to living together before he took the plunge.

"No problem." Todd reached for the remote

and turned down the volume. Dana bent and gave him a peck on the cheek before heading to the bedroom.

Todd felt totally bummed out as Dana shut the door behind her. There might as well have been an ocean between them instead of a thin plank of wood. He loved Dana so much, but ever since they moved in together, it was like he didn't know how to reach her anymore. He hoped it was just temporary—a bump in the road. But with each passing day it seemed like the gulf between them grew wider.

Suddenly he became aware of the faint strains of melancholy music floating over the sounds of baseball announcers and organ tunes. Todd muted the TV and listened attentively. The mournful notes seemed to vibrate with his own feelings, echoing every shade of his dark mood. Unexpectedly he felt something stirring deep within him.

The bittersweet melody drifted in a new direction, turning more sweet than bitter. Todd caught his breath as the exquisite vibrato became richer, fuller. He closed his eyes and felt his tension slip away as memories of tender moments with Dana surrounded him.

Beckoned irresistibly by the music, Todd got up and opened the bedroom door. Dana looked up in surprise, her bow frozen midnote. "Was I bugging you?" she asked.

"No, no, go on," Todd urged. "I just . . . it was just so beautiful."

Dana's face lit up. "You really think so?"

Todd nodded. "Normally I don't get into classical stuff, but that was . . ." He shook his head, unable to find the words. "*Wow*. So who wrote that—Beethoven? Mozart, one of those genius guys?"

Dana bit her lip and smiled. "Actually, I was improvising."

"You made that up?" Todd gasped.

"I was just playing out my feelings. I had a lot of pent-up emotions to vent." Dana's eyes were moist. "Feelings for you, Todd—that I can't communicate in words. The past few days have been so intense, it's like music was the only way to express what was in my heart."

Todd felt a lump welling in his throat. "Keep playing," he whispered, sitting down on the bed by Dana.

She lifted her bow and caressed the strings, the notes pouring forth with more clarity and certainty than before. There was still something wistful about the melody, but a note of pure joy shone through. Todd was transfixed as he watched Dana's slender hands flutter up and down the frets.

Dana's cello was spiraling into an awe-inspiring crescendo when there was a series of thumps on the bedroom wall. "Hey, keep it down in there!" a gruff, muffled voice snarled. Dana's bow faltered, and she smiled sheepishly at Todd.

Todd got up and took Dana in his arms—almost gingerly at first, as if she might pull away. When he felt her melt against him, he pressed her body hungrily to his. All at once Dana was laughing and crying and covering his face with kisses and Todd was kissing the tears away as they trickled down her face.

"I love you so much, Dana," he whispered. "Nobody's ever made beautiful music for me before."

Dana smiled through her sniffles. "I love you too, Todd. From now on, let's never be afraid to tell each other how we feel."

"It's a deal." He sealed it with an urgent kiss, unleashing all the emotion that had been trapped inside him for days. It felt so good to run his hands through Dana's hair, to inhale the scent of her skin. It felt like coming home.

"I have an idea," Todd murmured, pulling Dana down with him onto the bed. "Let's give the neighbors a *real* reason to complain about the noise."

"What's going on in here?" Jessica shouted over the incessantly throbbing bass of the stereo as she bounded down the stairs. Elizabeth and Neil were shouting while Sam and some jock type in a baseball cap were building what looked like a tower of cans, directly in front of the spot where she'd spent half an hour touching up smudges on the trim. "What is that atrocity blocking my gorgeous paint job?"

"Duuuude," the jock guy said, practically salivating as he glanced back and forth from Jessica to Elizabeth. "Either those tequila slammers last night were stronger than I thought, or . . . there's two of them."

Jessica stared at him. *Gross.*

"This is like a dream come true, dude," the guy said, rubbing his hands together. "Dude, *twins!*"

"Settle down, Floyd," Sam ordered, placing a hand on his buddy's shoulder.

"Jess, I'm glad you're here. Will you please back up me and Neil?"

"Sam actually considers that thing *art*," Neil explained, pointing an incriminating finger at the cans. "He must be stopped."

"My collection is staying," Sam declared, setting down two more cans.

"There must be some mistake." Jessica stared at Sam. "See, this is a *home,* not a junkyard. So you can pretty much forget about decorating it with garbage."

"Garbage?" Sam shook his head in disgust. "Oh, c'mon, Jess—I thought you of all people would be cool with somebody expressing their personality."

224

"Well, I don't want my home to express the personality of a frat-house basement," Jessica retorted. "Get that thing out of here or *else!*"

"Or else what?" Sam challenged. "You'll tell me I'm sporting all the wrong colors for fall?"

Floyd guffawed and shook his head in amusement. "Chicks, man. They're all the same and only good for—"

"*Chicks!* You—I—*rrr!*" Jessica was too angry to do more than sputter. Her hands were clenched into fists. She knew Sam wasn't exactly Mr. Sensitive, but she expected more from him than *that*. He knew she hated being thought of as shallow and superficial—that remark about fall colors was a cheap shot. And she couldn't even *begin* to address her issues with his Neanderthal friend.

"Don't disrespect Jess like that in our house!" Neil shouted to Floyd, moving protectively closer to Jessica. "You apologize right now!"

"Don't tell my friend what to do!" Sam shouted back. Jessica had forgotten what a stubborn jerk he could be.

"Well, your *friend* shouldn't be spouting sexist crap in the first place!" Elizabeth screamed. She had that look of pure rage in her eyes that both the twins got when one of them was being threatened. Jessica would feel touched if she wasn't so furious.

She tried to get a word in edgewise to defend

225

herself, but everyone was shouting at once. Jessica couldn't believe this scene was taking place in her own home. How had a few cans managed to wreak so much havoc in such a short time? As much as she hated to admit it, maybe Elizabeth was right—Sam *was* an impossible person to live with.

"I don't think I've ever seen so many stars," Chloe said as she and Tom emerged arm in arm from Oakley into the balmy twilight. "What a beautiful night."

"Hmmm," Tom agreed, looking up as if he were grateful to divert his attention. But Chloe didn't care. She was floating. Her heart was thumping in her chest. *Thumping*. She felt an exhilaration she hadn't experienced since the time she went skydiving. She still couldn't believe she'd actually had the guts to plant that monster kiss on Tom. The look on Moira's face was priceless.

As they walked to the parking lot, Chloe noticed again how incredibly cute Tom really was. He wore a white dress shirt and black pants. And, she knew from the kiss, he had on cologne. All of which meant he'd made an effort. For her!

Tom bent to unlock the car door and held it open for her. Chloe felt like a queen as she eased into the passenger seat. Well, the queen of Oakley Hall at least. She had her floor mates eating out of the palm of her hand. And everything was going great with Tom. Soon none of her stories about her boyfriend would be a lie. It was an incredible relief.

The funny thing was, she'd been so wrapped up in the facade with the Oakley girls that she hadn't even considered what it would be like to actually date her invented dream boyfriend. Tom was every bit as hot and sweet as she'd made him out to be. And it was obvious that he was in even better shape than when she'd met him last spring, his physique broadening into a quarterback's build. He was an incredible catch, just as she'd bragged. And as for the part about him being madly in love with her . . . well, that would come soon enough.

Tom started the car. "You do like Mexican, I hope. We can go somewhere else if—"

"Love it!" Chloe declared, an excited catch in her throat. He could have asked her if she liked eating dirt and she would have responded with equal enthusiasm. Whatever Tom was up for, Chloe was into it too. She hadn't gotten this far by being herself, so she wasn't going to start now.

The best part was that it was just a matter of time until she wouldn't have to pretend anymore about Tom. Pretty soon her fake relationship with everyone's dream man would be a reality.

*   *   *

"Sam, be reasonable!" Elizabeth's throat was hoarse from shouting over the pounding beat of the stereo. "Everyone else wants that heap of litter out of here!"

"Will you shut up about what everybody wants," Sam snapped. "Who died and put you in charge?"

"Don't talk to her like that!" Neil barked, jabbing his finger at Sam.

"Well, I don't have to toe your line either!" Sam's cocky smile was, for once, gone—but oddly enough, that brought Elizabeth no joy.

"You know, that rebel act gets old real fast." Neil's eyes held a kind of contempt Elizabeth had never seen in them. "Don't you ever get sick of going out of your way to piss people off?"

"Hey, I'm just being real," Sam retorted. "At least I'm not some uptight case who takes himself *waaay* too seriously!"

Elizabeth, stricken, stared back and forth between Sam and Neil as they went on arguing. As different as they were, the two guys had always gotten along fine over the summer. But they hadn't stopped yelling at each other for fifteen minutes. None of them had budged an inch.

"Listen, I don't care if it *is* your apartment," Floyd was saying to Jessica, waving a beer can. "I'm not about to take orders from some blond bimbo!"

"*Bimbo?*" Jessica shrieked. "That's nice talk from a slacker lunkhead."

228

"Bimbo!" Floyd growled.

"Jughead!" Jessica exclaimed.

"That is *it*." Floyd perched the beer can he was holding on the top of the pyramid. "Sorry, Sam, man, but I can't take another second in this insane asylum." He stomped to the front door.

As the door slammed behind Floyd, Sam turned on Jessica. "What did you say to my friend?"

Jessica planted her hands defiantly on her hips. "Why don't you ask that creep what *he* said to *me*?"

"Why don't you think twice before you bring a knuckle dragger like that guy into our house?" Neil interjected.

"Why don't *you* mind your own business?" Sam shot back.

Every nerve in Elizabeth's body felt jangled. This was insane. Nobody showed any sign of backing down—in fact, nobody was even talking sense. They were all just spewing insults at each other. She had to do something.

Elizabeth darted to the stereo and turned the music off. She breathed a sigh of relief. "You guys, could we all just sit down and talk about this like adults?"

All three of them turned on Elizabeth. "Stay out of this!" Sam and Neil said at the same time. Jessica just rolled her eyes.

"Well, I'm glad you agree on something,"

Elizabeth mumbled. As the others resumed squabbling, she felt tears of frustration spring to her eyes. This was a disaster! Sam hadn't even been here a day, and already they were all at each other's throats.

She had a sinking feeling that the beer-can pyramid was just the tip of the iceberg. After all, it wasn't like they'd been getting along great even before Sam moved in. All four of them had such strong, clashing personalities. How could they possibly exist peacefully under one roof?

Elizabeth groaned. It was going to be a long year.